FIRE ON

THE

MOUNTAIN

M.J. Rossi

FIRE ON THE THE MOUNTAIN

M.J. Rossi

HUDSON HOUSE

FIRST EDITION
ISBN 978-1-58776-963-4
Library of Congress catalog card number: 2015940812

Manufactured in the United States of America
NetPublications, Inc
675 Dutchess Turnpike, Poughkeepsie, NY 12603
www.hudsonhousepub.com (800) 724-1100

675 Dutchess Turnpike, Poughkeepsie, NY 12603
www.hudsonhousepub.com (800) 724-1100

FIRE ON THE MOUNTAIN

DEDICATION

To Our Children...
Colleen, Michael & Patrick

Always remember you are braver than you know, stronger than you seem, smarter than you think and loved more than you know...

INTRODUCTION

A mystery novel is a journey of endurance and speculation. You may have read my first novel, <u>Murder on the Mountain</u>. This novel, <u>Fire on the Mountain</u>, is a sequel BUT if you did not read the first book, do not worry!

Throughout <u>Fire on the Mountain</u> there are historical interludes and inspirational quotes to compliment the plot of the mystery. Writing can be a place of solitude. You owe it to yourself to find that peaceful place. I hope you enjoy this novel. Remember, reading helps us escape for a while…

PROLOGUE

"Hope Does Not Disappoint"

It was a ferocious fire. It was surprisingly fast moving. Even more so because the long standing home was predominantly made of stone. Life can change in a split second.

"I'm telling you, I know someone else is still inside the house!"

"How do you know?"

The black smoke could be seen for miles away. The house was located near the top of Hurricane Mountain in the Adirondacks. You could only get to the home by taking a mile long trail road.

"I'm telling you again, I know!"

The flames were shooting twenty to thirty feet above the roof. The fire chief of Essex County was on the scene as he lived at the base of the trail road. Chief Cameron was on his cell phone radioing for additional assistance even though he knew the house was already past saving. Over twenty volunteer firemen had arrived on the scene once the call was received. Many of them left their workplaces to assist with extinguishing the horrific blaze. It was as if the town had come to a standstill as so many people assisted. Their efforts, though, seemed futile. Suddenly there was a scream. It seemed to come from behind the house.

"Help! Help! Please help us!"

Three firemen ran to the back of the burning house. As they did so, a man leaped out the window he was seen screaming from. He landed partially on his right side. His head snapped back.

"I know who that is! What is he doing here?"

Off in the distance a person of small stature observed the scene. The individual watched for a while and then when it seemed like an appropriate moment, the individual departed down the trail. The person went away without anyone knowing.

ONE

"The way to get started is to quit talking and begin doing."

Edgar had been digging in his family's vegetable garden for the past two hours. He enjoyed tending to the crops he and his wife had planted. Their two daughters occasionally would check on the progress of the different vegetables but never really took a great interest as their father did. Edgar particularly liked being out in the yard when no one was home. He found solitude. But recently he became troubled and consumed with thoughts about the first family he had abandoned.

Edgar had once lived in Keene, a small hamlet in the Adirondacks in upstate New York. Even though he had only lived there for one year, he had made quite an impression on the residents of Keene. He had arrived there with his wife, Mary, and their two young sons, Michael and Ryan. Some people believed they had a daughter too, but she was never around. They had moved from Canada when Edgar Metcalf was appointed as the new minister of the regional Presbyterian Church.

His wife, Patricia, called out his name a few times before he realized she was trying to gain his attention.

"Edgar!" Patricia shouted a fourth time.

"Yes! I'm sorry, I did not hear you!"

"What's wrong? You look troubled. In fact, you are very pale," she said as she walked over to him.

Patricia put her arms around Edgar and she noticed he was sweating profusely.

"Are you alright? Your shirt is soaked with sweat and it's cool out here."

Edgar hesitated and then said, "No. No, I am fine. I guess I just got a little light-headed."

"Let's go inside."

He agreed but he knew that would not rid him of his anxiety about his abandoned family finding him and more importantly Patricia and their twin girls, Katherine and

Kelly, being betrayed and discovering his past life.

"Sit down Edgar. You look awful. Let me get you a glass of ice water."

Patricia went into the kitchen. Edgar noticed his hands were trembling. He folded his hands in his lap hoping his wife would not notice his shaking when she came back from the kitchen with the glass of water.

"Here Edgar, drink this slowly."

He did so. She sat across from him and knew she needed to probe and find out what was troubling her husband. Just last night he was talking in his sleep and murmuring odd statements such as,

"Stop.

"Leave us alone.

"How did you find me?"

Patricia knew something was awry. What was Edgar keeping from her? She began to feel uneasy. And she felt something was terribly wrong. What was Edgar not telling her about?

TWO

The volunteer firefighters did everything they could to salvage the home. Due to the speed of the fire, the Fire Chief suspected arson. But the fear of arson had become secondary as a grim discovery made the day even more dismal.

Three bodies were removed from the destroyed home. At first it was quite difficult to figure out if the first recovered body was a male or female as it was burned quite badly.

"I know who these people are."

"Who are they?" the Fire Chief asked.

"Bill, it's the Wilford family. The man who leaped from the back window is Todd Wilford."

The Chief said, "Oh no. His father was a good man. He always stopped by the fire station every Saturday morning with coffee

and donuts from the Stewarts Shop in
Keene."

The local newspaper's account was
gruesome:

"ARSON AND MURDER"

*"Our community has suffered a tragedy. A
home on Hurricane Mountain has burned to
the ground. But the riveting find has been
the discovery of three bodies in the fire's
remains. George Wilford, age 38, his wife
Janet Wilford, age 37 and their daughter,
Sabrina Wilford, age 16, were all found in
what was the living room of the home. Fire
Chief William Cameron has informed the
media that the three family members were
burned rather severely but they were also
each tied up and possibly gagged."*

Rita Smithly had written the account for the
local newspaper. She had never had to report
on such a horrific event as this fire, and she
had been reporting on local events for over
forty years. She found this assignment to be
particularly harrowing.

*"Initial reports have been made evident that
this fire is being treated as a criminal
investigation with possible murder charges*

*pending. As of this writing no suspects have
been identified. Funeral arrangements have
not been announced at this time for the three
Wilford family members. The lone known
survivor of the fire, Todd Wilford, the son of
George and Janet Wilford, remains in the
Elizabethtown Hospital. He is being
guarded by police security. "*

THREE

Edgar Metcalf had just received the awful news. His nephew, George Wilford and George's wife, Janet along with their daughter, Sabrina, had perished in a fire at their home on Hurricane Mountain. Edgar was also informed that their son, Todd, had survived the fire and was in Elizabethtown Hospital.

"Okay. I'll get there as soon as I can."

The caller then said, "Are you sure you want to do that?"

Edgar then said in somber fashion, "Yes. I know it's time I do so."

His wife, Patricia, was at the kitchen doorway as Edgar was finishing up with the telephone call.

"Who was that on the phone?"

"What?"

"Edgar, who were you speaking to on the phone?"

Edgar looked away at first but then walked over to her, held her right hand and said,

"Patricia, I need to talk to you. And I don't know how to begin."

"What is it Edgar? You know you can tell me anything."

Edgar hesitated but then responded, "I know. But this is rather difficult."

"Please, Edgar, you have me worried.'
"Patricia, I hope you still love me after I tell you something about me.'

Edgar wondered why he had made things so complicated. How could he hurt so many people he loved? What were his reasons? Patricia was a special person and he felt as if he ruined all they had. Patricia hugged Edgar and then she began to cry. Edgar knew he had to get things straightened out.

FOUR

The coroner had the grim task of performing the autopsies on the three Wilford family members. It was a rather gloomy day to begin with as James Boyler entered his office at eight o'clock in the morning. He was always the second to arrive as his secretary, Selma Griffin, greeted him with her pleasurable demeanor regardless of the circumstances around her at the coroner's office. Selma was rather used to the daily routine of the office as she had previously been the longtime secretary of the coroner before James Boyler. In fact, the townspeople always knew Selma was the one to maintain the office when Alexander Stevord was the coroner. Stevord was extremely unorganized and after his death, was found to be somewhat corrupt.

"Mr. Boyler, good morning."

"Good day Selma."

"Sir, you have two very important telephone messages. I placed them on your desk."

Boyler looked somewhat distracted but then responded to what Selma had just told him.

"Thank you. Who called?"

"Fire Chief Cameron called at 7:15. He said it was urgent."

"And who was the other caller?"

"Well, sir, the man did not identify himself."

Boyler looked at Selma. He hesitated to inquire more so, but then asked, "What did he say?"

"He told me you would most definitely want to speak to him immediately. He said, and I quote,

"'Have him call me before speaking to anyone else.' And then he gave me his telephone number and he hung up without saying goodbye."

Boyler could not even begin to speculate who it could possibly be. But he had to admit, he was intrigued by the mysterious call. He also knew without saying that the call was untraceable.

"Sir, would you like a cup of coffee?"

"No, Selma, I'm going to go into my office and decide who to call first. Please give me a few minutes."

"Okay, sir. I will close your door."

Boyler was quite overwhelmed. He was not looking forward to the three Wilford autopsies. And now he had to decide whether to call back the mysterious caller. Instead Boyler opted to call the Keene Police Chief Mark Winston. He knew he could seek his advice. Winston was known to have great knowledge of the many mysteries of the Adirondacks, particularly with murder cases. As did Winston, Boyler had thought his role in the Adirondacks would be somewhat laid back, but that was not the case as numerous troubling crimes had occurred in succession.

FIVE

Edgar asked Patricia to sit down so he could explain the conversation he had just completed on the telephone. Patricia knew something was wrong. She feared what Edgar was about to tell her would be startling. She did, though, anticipate Edgar had been hiding something.

"Please, Edgar, I'm worried. You look awful."

Edgar began by saying, "Patricia, I love you. I know you are wondering about the phone call. I need to explain to you about a situation."

Edgar was hesitating, but needed to continue. The front door opened. In came Kelly, one of their daughters.

"Mom. Dad. Are you here?"

Kelly walked into the kitchen.

"What's going on? Mom, you're crying!"

"Oh, Kelly…I'm okay."

Patricia asked Kelly to sit at the kitchen table.

"Dad, what's wrong? You look exhausted."

Edgar went over to Kelly and kissed the top of her head.

"Where is your sister?"

"Katherine is bringing in a few shopping bags."

Edgar quickly went outside to help Katherine. As soon as Edgar was out of the house, Kelly turned to her mother and asked,

"Mom, what is going on?"

"I'm not sure honey. Your Dad received a phone call and I have an awful feeling your Dad has some terrible news to tell us."

But Kelly did not seem to look surprised. She always felt her Dad was always mysterious about something.

"Kelly, how come you do not seem bothered?"

"Mom, I love Dad. And I always will but I think he will tell us what has always been bothering him. Don't worry, Mom. Everything will be alright."

"I hope so, honey. I hope so."

With that Edgar came back into the house with their other daughter, Katherine. Neither one was smiling.

SIX

**"For success, attitude is equally
important as ability."**

It was late afternoon when James Boyler had
completed all three of the autopsies. He
planned to meet with Police Chief Winston
at four thirty. Boyler had called Chief
Winston earlier this morning and Winston
told him he could meet with him later in the
day as he had a series of meetings he had to
attend.

Boyler was exhausted but he was also quite
concerned as he discovered each of the
Wilford family members had been murdered
before the fire had occurred. Both George
and Jane Wilford had been strangled. Their
hands and ankles had been tied up. Their
daughter, Sabrina, had been suffocated as a
noxious cloth was stuffed down her throat.
But Boyler was particularly perturbed as to
how the fourth family member, Todd

Wilford, not only escaped but had survived the brutal attacks on his family members. How was that possible? The fire commissioner's report stated that Todd Wilford had leaped from a back window. He did so even though both his hands and ankles were tied. Boyler found it rather unbelievable that Todd Wilford escaped with only minor bruises.

Boyler now knew he had more than one reason to meet with Keene Police Chief Mark Winston. Since Boyler had become the county coroner he took on quite a mess. The coroner's office had been run well by his secretary but the prior coroner, Alexander Stevord, did things as he wanted. His lack of protocol, or any for that matter, complicated quite a few cases that Boyler had to reopen and reinvestigate. Stevord's private wheeling and dealing was troubling. And now he had to handle the Wilford murder and arson case with great discretion. Something just did not seem right.

SEVEN

Edgar looked as though he had aged ten years in the last hour. His wife, Patricia, had become extremely concerned and somewhat agitated. And this was so out of character for her. What was he about to tell her?

"Patricia, I have much to tell you. And I don't know if you will be able to forgive me."

"Edgar, please, you are scaring me."

He knew he had done wrong by not being upfront with Patricia about his past life. How could he possibly tell her about the family he abandoned in Keene so many years ago? He suddenly left his wife and children. And now to complicate things, his nephew and wife, along with their daughter perished in a fire at their house on Hurricane Mountain. His nephew's son, Todd, had survived. Edgar was his oldest living relative. Supposedly he needed to reveal himself to the family he disappeared from to let them know he was alive and that the Metcalfs are related to the Wilfords. This was something his first wife, Mary, and their children knew nothing about.

Edgar had become absolutely overwhelmed by the entire situation. Everything seemed to be snowballing out of control. And now he realized he was about to devastate his second wife, Patricia, with such astounding information!

EIGHT

Before the coroner, James Boyler, met with Keene Police Chief Mark Winston, he released the findings of the three autopsy reports to the press. The details were harrowing:

- ☐ *George Wilford; male; 38 years old; died of a gunshot to the back of his head; his wrists and ankles had discolored from the extreme tightness of the ropes laced around his wrists and ankle; he died instantly.*

- ☐ *Janet Wilford; female; 37 years old; died of a gunshot to the right temple; her wrists and ankles were all broken; she died after her wrists and ankles were fractured; suffocation also evident.*

- ☐ *Sabrina Wilford; 16 years old; no injuries sustained other than*

suffocation from the extreme heat
from the fire; she burned to death.

Boyler summarized the reports; the details were gruesome. But he realized if he released the complete autopsy reports, the community would be overwhelmed, more so than what they were enduring right now. Upon completing the horrific task of releasing the reports to the press, Boyler took no questions. He then proceeded back to his office, closed the door and wept uncontrollably for close to thirty minutes.

NINE

"Bless me Father, for I have sinned." Edgar Metcalf was imagining himself entering a confessional and speaking to a priest, but he knew this could not be possible as he was not a practicing Catholic. His sense of guilt was weighing heavily on him. He then realized he was lying down on their living room couch. He could hear someone stirring in the kitchen. Was it Patricia? Had he told her the devastating news? If so, why couldn't he remember?

"Edgar, honey, are you awake?"

Edgar could not get himself to move off the couch.

Finally he responded, "Yes, I am awake." Again, Edgar tried to move and also could not recall if he told Patricia anything at all about his sudden disappearance he orchestrated years ago. Patricia came walking into the living room, sat down next to Edgar, and kissed him on the cheek.

Then she said, "Don't worry. Everything will be okay."

Edgar really did not know if he had informed Patricia and their daughters of his situation. Why was Patricia so calm? His abandonment of his first family so many years ago could not possibly be so accepted by Patricia. Something was not making sense. Was he dreaming?

TEN

James Boyler sat down at his desk to review the three autopsy reports he had completed. He wanted to make sure his accounts were properly detailed and legally aligned. What made this task even drearier is that he knew the Wilford family rather well. He had often gone hunting with George Wilford. Boyler was also lost in thought as he had an inclination, in fact a real belief, as to who killed George and Janet Wilford and their daughter, Sabrina, and then set the fast moving fire.

He became distracted when his secretary, Selma Griffin, knocked on his office door.

"Come in Selma."

"Sir, a gentleman is here to see you. He knows he does not have an appointment, but he says it is urgent."

"Did he say who he is?"

"Yes. His name is Edgar Metcalf."

Boyler suddenly looked ashen. Not much usually disturbed him but the hearing of Edgar Metcalf's name stunned him.

"Sir, are you alright?"

"Yes. No. Selma I think I need a glass of ice water."

Selma quickly departed Boyler's office and returned with a glass of ice water.

Boyler was already seated in a chair, nodded to Selma and asked her to tell Edgar Metcalf to have a seat and that he would meet with him momentarily.

James Boyler knew he needed to compose himself. He had never met Edgar Metcalf. He figured Selma knew who this man is and more than likely knew the story about his disappearance. Boyler was well aware of the lore of Keene. Residents had always talked through the years about the mysterious disappearance of Reverend Edgar Metcalf.

Boyler had a bad feeling about this. Should he contact police Chief Mark Winston? Or perhaps call one of Reverend Metcalf's two sons, either Ryan or the older brother, Michael, who lived in Lake Placid.

ELEVEN

The lawyer representing the Wilford family had just received an overnight package. It contained the detailed autopsy reports of George, Janet and Sabrina Wilford. He knew this would be a daunting task to read through the reports.

Hank Manson had been a lawyer for over forty years. He had not dread many days during his career, but this sadly was one of them. Manson began by perusing James Boyler's introductory notes; the notations were rather mundane but direct:

"The three bodies have been badly burned but I am able to identify each one. The details of each of the identifications will include age, gender, ethnicity, next-of-kin information, past medical history, and the circumstances that led to death.

"An autopsy was performed on each body. A technician was in the room to both witness the procedure and assist when necessary. Each body was cut open, body fluids were collected, and each internal organ was removed, weighed, examined and placed back into the body. Each body was sewn back up.

"Each autopsy performed has been video recorded. In addition, a series of digital photographs have been downloaded to the Essex County Coroner's data base. These images will substantiate the findings of this office.

"The three autopsies performed are based on the death investigation reports filed by the New York State Trooper Office. As per county ordinance, an autopsy must be completed due to potential homicide findings."

Manson was already overwhelmed by the generalizations in the autopsy report. He realized he was about to review the harrowing personal details of the Wilford family members' deaths. He figured it would be best to read the report in its entirety at this time. He continued:

[] *George Wilford; age 38; male; Caucasian; husband of Janet Wilford (deceased); father of Sabina Wilford (deceased); father of Todd Wilford (alive); cardiac history: heart attack suffered at age 35; fractured right leg at age 16; severe lacerations to both ankles and both wrists; rope lacerations around entire neck; died due to gunshot to the back of the head prior to fire; body identification confirmed with dental records.*

[] *Janet Wilford; age 37; female; Caucasian; wife of George Wilford (deceased); mother of Sabrina Wilford (deceased); mother of Todd Wilford (alive); asthmatic; cancer survivor (breast); breast cancer diagnosed at age 30; severe lacerations to both ankles and both wrists; died due to bullet shot to right temple and suffocation; broken neck; no sexual assault; body identification confirmed with dental records.*

[] *Sabrina Wilford; age 16; female; Caucasian; daughter of George and*

*Janet Wilford (both deceased); sister
of Todd Wilford (alive); asthmatic
since age three; two broken arms at
age ten (playground fall); lethal
levels of arsenic discovered in
bloodstream; died due to poisoning
and suffocation from fire; homicidal
poisoning suspected; no sexual
assault; body identification
confirmed with dental records.*

Hank Manson reviewed the digital
photographs the coroner had printed and
placed in the files. He could barely keep
control of his emotions. He had known the
Wilford family for many years. Who did
this? Why? And what did their son, Todd,
witness? Could he have done this? So many
thoughts ran through Manson's mind. He
knew he was dealing with a triple homicide,
more than likely first degree murders.

TWELVE

"A cloudy day is no match for a sunny disposition."

James Boyler had always wondered what happened to Edgar Metcalf. Due to all the talk over the years he truly never felt he died. He had some long conversations with his son, Ryan, and most recently with Edgar's grandson, Sean Metcalf. In addition, as usual, Selma had been able to provide a great amount of detail about Reverend Edgar Metcalf. Her memory of things of importance was absolutely amazing. Boyler exited his office.

"Good morning," Boyler said as he stretched out his hand to shake Edgar Metcalf's hand.

"Good day, Mr. Boyler, I'm..."

"I know who you are," replied Boyler in a curt manner. Boyler's demeanor was quite out of character, but no one could blame him.

"Mr. Boyler, I am here to explain myself."

"It's not me you owe an explanation."

"But I need your help."

"I don't think so."

"Well, sir, I am old and I'm dying." Boyler did not show any emotion after Metcalf made such a statement.

Metcalf continued, "Please, sir, I am in need of assistance."

Suddenly the front door of the coroner's office flew open. Standing before James Boyler, his secretary Selma Griffin and Edgar Metcalf, were Ryan and Sean Metcalf along with a uniformed police officer.

Upon seeing his son and grandson, Edgar Metcalf fell to the floor and began to cry. No one at first knew how to react. Was Edgar being dramatic or was he truly overwhelmed by everything happening around him.

THIRTEEN

The funeral for the three Wilford family members had been delayed for almost two weeks. This was not only due to the autopsies being performed but also some of the family members and longtime friends needed to travel quite a distance to arrive in Keene.

The people of Keene had been devastated by the deaths of George and Janet Wilford and their daughter, Sabrina. The Wilford's son, Todd, had been released from the hospital and decided to stay with the Metcalf family. The residents of Keene had once again rallied to assist one of their own. Just last year they had shown their support for both the Metcalf and Hamilton families after bizarre murder charges were placed against Sean Metcalf. He had been accused of murdering Matthew Hamilton. Due to startling evidence, the charges were dropped.

The little church in Keene was packed as the funeral service began. It was a cool, crisp, clear day. It was not the least bit humid. The priest, Father Devon, put forth a beautiful mass. Todd Wilford was able to present a short but eloquent eulogy on behalf of his deceased family. Todd is a strapping young man, fifteen years of age. People often thought he was older.

He began, "Thank you for being here today. Thank you, Father Devon for the mass service. Your words of comfort help my family, friends and I to get through this tragedy. I would like to read a passage my Dad believed in and I feel it will comfort us too."

Todd took a deep breath, looked out at the congregation and read the passage with great poise,

"Storms may chase us, and our plans may be knocked off course, yet God will be there to guide us.

We can choose to abandon ship. But we should not.

We can become hardened. But we shall not.

We can rely on the Lord. He may use us as beacons of hope where it is least expected. Hope does not disappoint."

Todd stepped away from the podium, bowed before the altar and returned to his pew where Sean Metcalf embraced him. Father Devon stood; the congregation did likewise.

Father Devon then spoke,

"Todd, that was very special. Your Dad would be proud of you."

You could hear a few people crying; one person, in particular, was sobbing at the back doorway, but the individual departed before the priest completed the funeral mass.

Father Devon said, "Let us pray…." With that the ceremony was concluded.

The people left the church and proceeded to the Keene Cemetery. Even though it was only a short distance away, it took quite a while to begin the prayer service for the Wilford family members as over 60 vehicles made their way to the cemetery grounds. In addition, a good number of people walked to the cemetery.

Father Devon recited a series of prayers and then the friends followed by the family members placed carnations and roses on the three coffins. It was a harrowing, numbing experience for all in attendance. Todd sat silently with tears streaming down his face. One of his uncles sat to his right with his arm around Todd's shoulder. Sean was at Todd's other side.

Family and friends slowly departed and went to the Metcalf home where a large tent had been set up along with numerous long tables. The tables contained many trays of food for everybody to indulge in. Todd was overwhelmed by the outpouring of support.

Off to the side of the tent was an elderly gentleman along with a lady. One of the Hamilton family members recognized the man, walked up to him and said rather loudly,

"Is that you? Are you Edgar Metcalf?"

FOURTEEN

"ARREST!"

This was the full page headline. But this was already old news to the local residents picking up the Lake Placid newspaper. A person of great interest had been arrested for the murders of the three Wilford family members.

"After (only) three weeks of high anxiety and tenseness in the hamlet of Keene and the surrounding area, an arrest has been made of the person suspected of committing arson thus resulting in the deaths of George Wilford, age 38, his wife, Janet Wilford, age 37 and their daughter, Sabrina, age 16. Their bodies had been discovered in the remnants of their home. It is believed they each had been murdered prior to the fire which destroyed the Wilford home.

Eric Dolloy, age eighteen, has been charged with a series of felony counts, including arson and first degree murder. His alibi does not seem to substantiate his whereabouts. Dolloy did inform police he had been scorned by Sabrina Wilford after being her boyfriend for the past six months.

Dolloy has been detained at the county jail in Elizabethtown. A bail hearing is scheduled for this afternoon. It is expected that Dolloy will plead not guilty for all the charges filed against him. Once again, this region has suffered a devastating tragedy."

FIFTEEN

"Come in."

"Thank you."

"We've been expecting you. You know we are angry but also curious as to why you are here."

The elderly man did not seem to know what to do next. Then he was asked if he and his wife would like to sit down. They did so. Then they were offered cups of coffee. They graciously accepted.

There was an odd sense of silence among all of them. After quite a few moments, which seemed much longer, Sean Metcalf was the first to say something.

"Grandpa, why are you back in Keene? And why did you leave so long ago?"

Edgar Metcalf looked at his wife, Patricia. Then he looked back over to his grandson, Sean, and his son, Ryan.

"I do not know where to begin." Rita Metcalf, Ryan's wife, handed Reverend Metcalf and his wife cups of coffee. Edgar took a sip and then began,

"I am terribly sorry for any grief I caused. I know it has been a long time. And I am sure you have many questions." He bowed his head down. He spoke very slowly and quietly. Suddenly, the front door flew open. A man appeared who looked very much like Edgar.

"You are right about that!" yelled Michael Metcalf. "You have some nerve coming back here!"

"Michael," said Ryan, "Wait a minute. Let's hear him out!"

Michael paced the room. Edgar's wife, Patricia, began to cry quietly. She knew this would be an extraordinary encounter but this was quite overwhelming. How could it not be! She stood up and was embraced by Edgar's first wife, Mary, Michael and Ryan's mother.

Mary then turned to Edgar and simply said,

"Edgar, I am a woman of great faith. Surely, you must have had just cause for your actions."

Edgar began to speak, stood up and then passed out!

SIXTEEN

Mark Winston, the Keene Police Chief, had
an uneasy feeling about the arrest of Eric
Dolloy for the murders of the three Wilford
family members. Dolloy seemed to
contradict his statements. Even though he
was connected with Sabrina Wilford as a
boyfriend, that did not necessarily mean he
had set the Wilford house on fire after he
allegedly had murdered the Wilfords. Where
was the evidence?

Dolloy, during intense questioning, at first
stated all four Wilford family members were
killed. Dolloy also seemed to be so angry
about his recent and sudden break up with
Sabrina Wilford that he went hiking on one
of the Forty-Sixer trails of the High Peaks.
His best friend, Adam Williams, ventured
the trail with him. This occurred on the day
of the fire. Prior to Dolloy's arrest, Williams
had not been questioned by the police.
Winston questioned how it came to be that

Dolloy was arrested for something he may not have been in the area when it occurred. Adam Williams was able to state that Dolloy was with him on the trail at the time of the fire at the Wilford home. In fact, Dolloy and Williams were near the top of the summit of Mount Marcy when the horrific crimes had occurred.

Chief Winston, rightfully so, felt a more thorough investigation needed to be done. Ironically, this tragedy took place at the same time Reverend Edgar Metcalf unexpectedly reappeared after being away from Keene for so many years. Winston always thought his job as the Keene Police Chief would be quiet and calm; that was quite the contrary.

Winston left his office and made his way to Ryan Metcalf's home. He needed to tap into Detective Metcalf's astute investigative prowess. Winston knew Ryan Metcalf could remain professional even though it was an emotional time for him and his family.

SEVENTEEN

"Ryan, I hope I'm not disturbing you."

"No, Mark, I could use the distraction. My father's return has taken a toll on all of us."

"Thank you for seeing me at this time."

Mark Winston continued by saying, "As you know we are struggling with the arson and murder case. The Wilford's son, Todd, has surely been eliminated as a suspect."

"Why?"

"Well, he also was tied up. Did you not know that?"

"You mean he leaped from the window with his hands tied behind his back?

"Yes."

"So, do you have any suspects?"

"Well, as you know a person has been arrested, but I have real doubts. So, no, not at this time, but I have some suspicions."

Mark Winston seemed even more exhausted than Ryan Metcalf. Who could blame either one of them with all the turmoil taking place in Keene.

"You seem hesitant about sharing information. Is that true?"

"No, Mark, I'm at a standstill. Whoever committed the three murders and then torched the Wilford home has seemed to unbelievably leave behind no traces or clues."

"Did you speak to the Wilford's son, Todd, to question him about any people who did not get along with his family? And who tied him up? He must know that or at least be able to give a description of the individual."

"He only rambled on about how everyone loved his family. He said he was grabbed from behind, blindfolded and dropped to the floor without seeing the perpetrator nor hearing a voice."

"What about his sister, Sabrina? Did she have a boyfriend? Maybe there was an acquaintance or a close friend?"

"Well, Mark, I have not really pursued that line of questioning. But I should."

"I would interview Todd Wilford more in depth. I'm sure he could provide some valuable insights, even if he remembers some details he may have not realized immediately after the murders of his family."

Ryan got up from his chair and walked over to the window. The view was stunning. Ryan was looking out at the beautiful scenery of some of the High Peaks of the Adirondacks. Ryan became very quiet.

"Ryan, are you alright?"

Ryan hesitated then he said, "Why did my father come back? I would have preferred he remained missing, even though I know Sean was looking for him. Sean always thought, even at a young age, that my father was alive."

"Well, I need to tell you something."

EIGHTEEN

**"Success is a ladder you cannot climb
with your hands in your pockets."**

The news spread throughout Keene in quick
fashion. Memories had been recalled about
past sensational murders that took place in
this small hamlet and the surrounding area.
Keene is a close knit community but has
dealt with some bizarre murder mysteries
the past few years.

"Thank you for being here. We have made
an arrest regarding the Wilford family
homicides."

The crowd of people listened attentively to
the mayor's statements. Standing behind her
was Police Chief Winston. The most recent
mayor, Simon Galente, had passed away two
months ago due to an unfortunate hunting
accident in nearby Saranac Lake.

She continued, "All evidence supports that the three Wilford family members were murdered prior to their home being torched. The arrested individual is being charged with numerous felony counts including kidnapping, arson and homicide."

The mayor paused for a few moments before turning the podium over to Police Chief Winston.

"Chief Winston will give you some further details. Please be patient as we can only share so much information without jeopardizing the case." The new mayor, Donna Galente, seemed uncomfortable being in the limelight. She seemed somewhat nervous and distracted. She had only recently been appointed mayor, after the death of her husband, Simon Galente. Many townspeople had persuaded her to complete her husband's term. After much pondering, she did so reluctantly. Whoever thought she would have such a dramatic situation to tackle.

"Good morning," said Chief Winston.

He continued, "I am unable to share many details at this time. I can tell you that the person we have arrested is Milton Brownfield."

There was a loud murmur throughout the gathered group. They all thought Eric Dolloy had been arrested. Was this an additional arrest? Was Dolloy released?

Winston asked the crowd to quiet down before he resumed.

"We have arrested Milton Brownfield, the past co-owner of the Lake Placid Miniature Golf establishment. As some of you may know, he is a relative of the Wilford family. And we have released Eric Dolloy as there is no credible evidence against him. I have no further details or comments at this time."

Both Mayor Galente and Police Chief Winston left the podium without taking any questions from the media. Mayor Galente leaned over to Chief Winston and mentioned to him that the case seemed very complicated. Winston then said to her to expect the unexpected.

The crowd was both startled and dumbfounded. How could the murderer be Milton Brownfield? He is George Wilford's nephew and had just moved in with the

Wilford family? Did Todd Wilford have anything to do with this horrific situation? And why was Eric Dolloy released so quickly? The townspeople, in general, were rather skeptical. Were the mayor and police chief holding back vital information?

NINETEEN

Edgar Metcalf had a tremendous amount of explaining to do. After being assisted to the couch and given a glass of water, Edgar was able to start his explanation of his whereabouts.

"Ryan, I realize you are angry with me and you have every right to be."

"What do you expect? My mother has suffered horrifically so these past few years. Look at her!"

"Do you think that is why I came back? I know your mother has suffered! And it's my fault."

Edgar hesitantly looked away and then looked back up at all of them. He continued to speak, "Your mother knew I was not happy here."

"What excuse is that? You just left us. You left behind Mom, Michael, and Josephine who we hardly ever see since she was institutionalized. As well, as myself! Did you know Josephine, your daughter, has not allowed us to have contact with her in years? Did you know I have a wonderful wife and son? Did you know Michael won't ever talk about you? And did you know my son, Sean, your grandson, is probably the most intelligent of all us as he felt you were alive?"

Ryan could barely contain himself. He wanted to physically lash out at his father. Everybody in the room knew this was a side of Ryan that rarely was exhibited. A door opened up. Everyone looked to see who entered the Metcalf house.

"Hello Father. I am here but not to speak to you. Ryan, I need to see you outside on the front porch." Sean and his mother, Rita looked over to Mary who had turned very pale. The visitor was Josephine. Mary began to weep but was too weak to go out onto the porch and greet her long lost estranged daughter.

TWENTY

Milton Brownfield awaited his arraignment. He was rather disheveled and had had nothing to eat in the last few hours as he had no appetite whatsoever. He had no family as well in the area other than Todd Wilford, his cousin. He also could not afford an attorney. He only said one thing to the police officers since he was arrested, "I have to speak to Todd Wilford."

But Milton's requests were ignored. In fact, at one point Milton got visibly upset and started to scream over and over, "He's the only person I will speak to!"

The arresting officer finally spoke to Milton and asked him a question.

"What about your uncle?"

Milton looked confused. Then he said, "You mean my Uncle George? He's alive?"

"No."

"Who are you talking about?"

The officer hesitated to respond. He walked away and Police Chief Mark Winston came to the jail cell area.

"Milton, how are you holding up?"

Milton did not respond. He looked down at the jail cell floor.

"Your uncle is here. Uncle Edgar. The reverend has asked to see you."

Milton looked up. He was startled. What is going on? Out loud Milton screamed, "I thought he was dead!"

"He's not. He returned to Keene. Are you aware of his past?" asked Chief Winston.

Milton looked too baffled to speak.

"Do you want to see him?"

Milton could only nod. He was exhausted. Winston left to go get Reverend Metcalf.

TWENTY ONE

Todd could not believe what had happened. How did they decide to arrest Milton? Then he thought out loud, "They'll probably come for me…"

A car pulled into Sean and Sabrina Metcalf's driveway. Todd had been staying with them and their young son, Ryan, since Todd was released from the hospital. Todd looked out the living room window. It was raining rather hard so Todd knew the police car would pull up to the doorway as the gravel driveway led right up to the house. No one else was home except for Todd. He knew he would have to open the door as Sean's newly bought used pickup truck was in the driveway and the hood was probably still warm. He knew he did not have a license but Sean let him drive the truck just the same.

Todd decided to open the door before the officer knocked.

"Hello Todd."

"Hello sir."

"Todd, I need to speak with you. Is anyone else here?"

"No sir."

"May I come in?"

"Yes sir."

Todd felt he had no choice but to let the officer come inside the house. Once inside, the officer turned to Todd and said,

"How are you doing?"

"Fine sir"

"How have you been holding up?"

Todd thought to himself why was the officer asking such questions and did he really care.

"Fine."

Todd did not want to appear nervous or reluctant to answer the officer's questions.

"Todd, are you aware of Milton Brownfield being arrested?"

"Yes."

"Do you know what for?"

"Yes."

Again Todd was reluctant to give up much information.

"Do you think he killed your Mom, Dad and sister?"

"Why are you asking me these questions?"

Suddenly the front door opened and Sean Metcalf walked in.

"Sean," said the officer. "How are you?"

"Fine. Officer Tedesco, what are you doing here?"

"I came to speak to Todd."

Sean looked over at Todd and said, "Todd, come with me."

Todd and Sean walked into the kitchen and spoke for a few minutes.

"Todd, I am telling you to not say a word to the cop. Do you hear me?"

"Yes, but..."

"But what?"

"Never mind."

Todd and Sean walked back into the living room but Officer Tedesco had already left.

"Sean, what's going on?"

"I don't know, Todd, you tell me."

TWENTY TWO

Immediately after Officer Tedesco left, another car drove up to Sean's house. There were three people; Sean recognized all of them. Sean's father, Ryan, exited the car first followed by Sean's grandfather, Edgar Metcalf, who suddenly reappeared in Keene, along with Edgar's second wife, Patricia. Things were becoming complicated.

Sean decided to open the front door before the three car occupants even approached the house.

"Good morning Sean," his Dad said.

"Hi Dad. What's going on?"

"Is Todd here?"

"Yes."

"Well. Your grandfather needs to speak to him."

Todd appeared at the doorway. He looked older than his age but he also looked rather frazzled.

Todd then spoke up.

"Hello. What do you want? Sean told me you are my uncle?"

Edgar came up the stairs to the house and embraced Todd. Todd reluctantly hugged him back. Then Edgar could be heard saying to him,

"People believe you murdered your family." Edgar then paused a few moments and then said, "Did you?"

Todd tried to wriggle away from Edgar. As he did so, Edgar fell backwards, hit his head and was unconscious. Todd was startled and ran down the driveway.

TWENTY THREE

Milton reluctantly gave his account to the police officer as to what had occurred the night of the fire at the Wilford house. Milton's recall of the events alluded to the possibility that Todd Wilford had planned the murders of his parents and sister. The summary of Milton Brownfield's testimony was harrowing. Police Chief Winston reviewed it with such a painful expression on his face. It read as follows:

"Milton, it is my understanding you're willing to freely give an account of the happenings at the Wilford house?"

"Yes."

(In the notes of the report it stated Milton Brownfield's court appointed lawyer was present).

"Were you at the Wilford house the night of the fire?"

"Yes."

(It is also noted the police officer conducting the inquiry was Officer Tedesco).

"Besides George and Janet Wilford and their daughter, Sabrina Wilford, was anyone else present at the household with you?"

"Yes, Todd Wilford."

"What did he do that night?"

"What do you mean?"

"Please tell me if he did any harm to his family."

(It is noted Milton glanced over to his lawyer seated next to him. His lawyer just nodded affirmatively. Milton hesitated for a few moments and then responded.)

"Yes...he asked me to go into the shed to look for a tank of gas. He said it should be on the right side once I got into the shed. He said we needed it to get the tractor ready for cutting the fields the next day."

"Did you not think that was kind of odd to do at night time?"

"It was right after dinner."

"So Milton, did you find the gas tank?"

"Yes."

"What did you do with it?"

"Todd asked me to go to the local gas station to fill it up."

"Did you?"

"Yes."

"I thought you were not of age to drive at that time. Is that correct?"

(It is noted Milton reluctantly answered the question by simply saying, "Yes sir.")

Chief Winston noted Officer Tedesco had continued his questions by asking Milton what he did when he arrived back at the house. Milton explained,

"I went upstairs to see Todd. When I opened his bedroom door Todd was covered in blood."

"What did you do?"

"I ran over to him to see what happened."

"What did he tell you?"

"He could barely speak. I kept asking him…"

A knock occurred at Winston's office door. He opened the door and standing before him was Ryan Metcalf. He looked somber.

"Mark, my father, Edgar, is dead."

TWENTY FOUR

**"Anything unattempted remains
impossible."**

Patricia, Edgar's second wife, was at the
town of Upper Jay funeral home making
arrangements for Edgar's wake. The series
of events during the last few days were
rather grim and also bizarre.

"Mrs. Metcalf, Edgar had pre-arranged his
funeral. The costs were paid years ago when
he was a minister in this area."

"Yes, I am aware of that."

"Do you want to abide by his wishes?"

"Yes, please."

"Do you realize he wanted to be cremated?"

"Yes."

"He also set aside a cemetery plot for yourself, your daughters, along with his first wife Mary, and his children from his first marriage and any grandchildren."

"What? I don't understand."

"I think you need to read his revised will that was notarized last week."

"Oh, my…"

Patricia looked rather pale. The funeral director asked her if she would like a glass of water or a cup of coffee.

"No thank you. I just need to go outside for some fresh air."

Patricia walked outside to a beautiful garden. She sat down on a wooden bench that looked out over the mountains of Upper Jay. The view was spectacular. It seemed to give some solace to Patricia.

There was some noise behind Patricia.

"Mom, we've been looking for you."

Standing beside Patricia were her two daughters.

"Oh, dear, your father has made such a mess of things."

TWENTY FIVE

"It is with great sorrow we are gathered here today to say goodbye to Reverend Edgar Metcalf."

The congregation was rather large; people were overflowing outside the Presbyterian Church. Many were in attendance as there was great curiosity since Edgar Metcalf returned to Keene. It was not unusual to hear people discussing the odd circumstances of his reappearance.

The minister continued,

"Edgar Metcalf had a good heart. His return to our community has had a great and profound effect on many of us. God always watches over us, even in times of distress."

Seated in the front row on the right side of the church were members of Edgar Metcalf's first family. His children Ryan and Michael along with their mother, Mary, his first wife sat together. Mary's other child, Josephine, was not in attendance. Her whereabouts was always a gossiped item by the townspeople of Keene. Mary had suffered a stroke and needed a cane to assist her with walking. Also in the second pew were Edgar's grandson, Sean, along with his wife, Sabrina. Ryan's wife, Rita, a very solemn and religious woman, refused to attend the service.

"As we mourn his loss, we need to remember to forgive his decisions that were not meant to hurt anyone. He truly did not intend to bring about such dissension. Yet, we know, his unfortunate death has left so many unanswered questions. Sometimes God is not able to provide us with answers to every mystery in life."

Reverend Metcalf's second family was seated on the left side of the church. His second wife, Patricia, along with her two daughters, Katherine and Kelly, on each side of her had their heads bowed down through practically the entire funeral service. In addition, Patricia's two sons-in-law were in attendance. Each couple had two children; all four of them sat in the second pew.

Patricia could be heard sobbing at different times.

Oddly enough, Todd Wilford decided to sit in the last pew at the back of the church.

The weather outside was dreadful. The cold rain was not a concern though for people standing outside under umbrellas. The service was not too long as the minister concluded with the final prayer by asking everyone to abide by the Lord's command of loving one another and to love thy neighbor.

The attendees departed the church and many proceeded to the Upper Jay cemetery. As expected, practically every person decided to attend the graveside ceremony. The rained had subsided and the sun was beginning to peek out from behind the clouds. But three people decided to not attend the ceremony: Ryan and Michael Metcalf and their mother, Mary.

Michael could be heard saying, "That man was such a bastard."

His mother said solemnly, "Please, Michael, do not curse. He is dead and he can no longer harm us."

TWENTY SIX

Milton Brownfield had been released from jail as there had not been enough evidence, beyond a reasonable doubt, to charge him with three counts of murder along with arson. Milton did not attend Edgar Metcalf's funeral service but he was on the hillside overlooking the Upper Jay cemetery. Milton was surprised the police did not detain him because he thought he would be considered some sort of an accomplice or the actual murderer. Maybe they felt he had absolutely nothing to do with the horrific murders. Or maybe they were trying to set him up. He thought to himself they may be trying to trap him since he was at the Wilford house. No one may ever be able to prove if he committed such a crime.

The crowd of people attending the cemetery service was overwhelming. Milton was sure the people of this area had never witnessed such an outpouring for a funeral. There were more in attendance at the graveside than were at the church. Edgar Metcalf was simultaneously loved and hated by the people of the region. One person Milton was fearful of was Edgar Metcalf's nephew, Todd Wilford. Even though Milton was in fine physical shape, and a year older than Todd, he was concerned Todd would seek him out and harm him, or possibly kill him. He knew Todd better than anyone and knew what he was truly capable of doing.

Milton looked down at the crowd and turned to see if he could spot Todd. A rustling of the wind startled Milton somewhat but then he gazed down at the assembled crowd. Suddenly there was a tap on Milton's shoulder. Milton swung around quickly and standing before him was Todd Wilford.

Todd looked rather imposing to Milton. Todd was sweating rather profusely yet he had a grin on his face.

"Did you not expect me?"

Milton tried to respond back calmly,

"Todd, what's going on?"

"Milton, let's take a walk."

TWENTY SEVEN

After the last week of frantic activity with the death and burial of Edgar Metcalf, Police Chief Winston reviewed the account of Milton Brownfield's statements. It had become clear to Winston that it was only the proper thing to authorize the release of Milton Brownfield from jail. He could not have and did not murder the Wilford family members. Nor was he an accomplice. But did he provide information to implicate someone else?

Officer Tedesco entered the police station and proceeded to the police chief's office.

"Sir, do you have a minute?"

"Sure. Come in."

Tedesco was a gentle giant. Even though his physical size could intimidate almost anyone, Tedesco was calm and professional as he conducted himself with police matters.

"Sir, a body has been discovered at the ravine in Upper Jay by the covered bridge by the cemetery."

"Has an identification of the body been made?" asked Chief Winston.

"Not yet sir, but it may have something to do with the Wilford homicide case."

"Why is that?"

Officer Tedesco hesitated and then said, "Well, sir, I think you need to go to the site. It is very troubling."

TWENTY EIGHT

Even though Edgar Metcalf's burial had taken place three days ago, crowds of people continued to stream to the gravesite. It was a rather harrowing scene. The staff at the Upper Jay cemetery was overwhelmed by the vehicles that continued to frequent the cemetery. Even though Edgar Metcalf had only lived in Keene for one year so long ago, there was still the odd circumstances of his disappearance that kept so many people wondering and speculating about him.

And now news broke that a body had been discovered at the ravine by the area of Edgar Metcalf's grave marker.

The people of Upper Jay had never experienced such chaos. Jay is a rather small rural area consisting of approximately 2400 people. Because of the rugged terrain, much of the hamlet of Jay is undeveloped. Tourists are attracted to the area because of the scenic beauty, the wilderness and the peacefulness.

But all that seemed to be shattered as these events had upset the community. It seemed to be wherever Edgar Metcalf visited controversy or turmoil of some sort seemed to occur.

TWENTY NINE

Todd Wilford had decided to drive Sean's vehicle to Saranac Lake. No cop would stop him if he kept to the speed limit. He would be sixteen in a couple of weeks. He had no driver's license. But since he looked much older than fifteen, he knew he could drive and not be stopped. He did though feel bad about taking Sean's car without permission.

As he drove out of the driveway, he took a right turn. He looked in the rear view mirror and saw Sean's wife's car coming up the road. How could he explain taking Sean's car. Todd knew he was considered a prime suspect of killing his family. And now Milton Brownfield has caused total chaos. Milton was supposedly his best friend. Why did he cause such a dilemma by telling the police so much information?

Todd realized he had to get away to figure out what was going to happen. Todd thought to himself that he had no choice but to confront Milton. And Milton just made things more difficult for him, but he had to do what he did. Milton obviously did not want to listen to him and help out. Todd knew Saranac Lake would be a safe haven.

Todd also knew Milton would no longer be a concern of his.

THIRTY

"Being willing makes you able."

Police Chief Winston and Officer Tedesco arrived at the ravine by the Jay covered bridge. Numerous emergency vehicles had already descended upon the scene. A body had been pulled from the stream.

Winston walked over to the gurney. He turned to the county coroner, James Boyler, and asked for an update.

"Hello Mr. Boyler."

"Good afternoon Chief."

"Could you provide me with an update?"

"Yes sir. We have removed a body from the stream by the covered bridge. The victim is a female. At this time I believe the cause of death is drowning."

"Do you know who it is?"

"Yes. It is Mary Metcalf."

The police chief looked over at Officer Tedesco and nodded his head.

"Do you believe there was any foul play?"

"No sir. But I'll be performing an autopsy to officially declare a cause of death."

The police chief turned to Officer Tedesco and asked,

"Why was Mary Metcalf here?"

Chief Winston waited for a response from Tedesco, but he remained quiet.

Then Winston asked Tedesco, "But why come here? She lives in Keene. Her car is here so she must have driven here."

"Sir, a report says a car looking similar to Sean Metcalf's, stopped here a few hours ago and dropped Mary Metcalf off."

Winston and Tedesco walked back over to their vehicle. Winston put out an alert on Sean Metcalf's car. He then drove to Sean's house. Upon arriving, he knocked on the door. Within a few moments, Sean opened the door.

Winston greeted Sean, "Sean, how are you?"

"Fine, thank you."

"Is your wife out?"

"No, she is here."

"Does your Dad have your car?"

Sean hesitated. Winston followed by asking,

"Where is your car?"

Again, Sean hesitated.

"Sir, I'm not sure."

"Sean, I need to ask you if Todd Wilford is here."

"No sir."

"Do you think he has your car?"

"I hope not. He's not even sixteen yet."

Winston radioed to Tedesco.

"Put out an alert on Todd Wilford. He may be driving a Honda CRX vehicle, grey, license plate 234-ART."

"Roger, sir."

Winston turned to Sean and said,

"I need you to sit down Sean. I need to tell you something."

Sean let out with a wailing sound upon hearing of the news of his grandmother, Mary Metcalf.

THIRTY ONE

Todd turned into the Best Western Hotel parking lot in Saranac Lake. He decided to call Milton and have him meet him.

"Milton, I want you to do what I told you."

"Now?"

"Yes, now. Meet me at the place I told you about. Do not come with anyone else."

There was silence on the other end of the cell phone.

"Milton, do you hear me?"

"Yes."

"Leave now."

"Okay." Then Todd disconnected the call.

Milton decided to get into his car and made his way to Saranac Lake. He could arrive there in thirty minutes. When he got to the parking lot of the hotel, he spotted Sean

Metcalf's car that Todd had been driving, but Todd was nowhere to be found. Milton got out of the car. It was dark by now, approximately ten o'clock.

Milton got out of his car and walked over to the vehicle. A person came out from behind the car and looked at Milton.

"Come with me."

"Where are we going?"

"Follow me. I have a gun and I'll use it. Do you understand?"

Milton looked worried but did not panic.

"Go into that alley way. I'm right behind you."

The area was dimly lit. Todd's hand was shaking and Milton realized he made a mistake by coming here. Milton suddenly turned around and confronted Todd.

"You are making things worse. The cops are looking for you!"

"For what?"

"Mary Metcalf's body was found."

"What?"

"You are suspected of doing something. The car you were driving was seen at the covered bridge."

"That's not possible."

"Todd, I know you killed your family."

'No! No Milton." Todd seemed to be losing control of his temper.

He continued to yell, "You did it Milton! You brought the gas into the house! You tied them up! You murdered them!"

Milton knew Todd was out of control; he feared Todd might use the gun.

A loud noise occurred down the alley way. Both Todd and Milton looked in that direction. Todd then grabbed Milton from behind and began to choke him. Milton was overpowered by Todd and passed out. Todd then pulled Milton's body into the bushes and departed. He did not think anyone saw what had happened. Todd was in an anxious state of mind and did not know what to do next.

Todd knew it would seem like he did something wrong if he continued to run away from the situation. He knew himself he did not kill his family and yet he could not prove he saw Milton do so as Milton had blindfolded him as things became chaotic at the house. And now who would believe him. Milton was trying to blame him for the murders of his mother, father and sister.

THIRTY TWO

The Saranac Lake Police Department had received a phone call from the Keene police chief, Mark Winston, alerting them about Todd Wilford's possible appearance in Saranac Lake. The police relayed an all-points bulletin with a description of both Sean Metcalf's car and Todd Wilford: 6'2"; 210 pounds; brown hair; blue eyes; 15 years old (looks 18); dressed in jeans, black short sleeved shirt and sneakers. In addition, the report stated Todd Wilford may be armed.

A ruckus was occurring at the Best Western Hotel in Saranac Lake. Upon arriving at the parking lot, numerous teenagers were scattering the area. A body was found in the bushes. The individual was gagged and was breathing. The person was able to speak and identify himself as Milton Brownfield. Milton proceeded to report of his confrontation with Todd Wilford. The police continued their search for Todd Wilford.

101

A Saranac Lake police officer began to ask Milton questions.

"Milton, did he say where he was going?"

"No."

"Why did you come here?"

"He asked me to do so."

"Did he tell you anything of importance?"

"No."

"Why did he try to strangle you?"

Milton hesitated, then said,

"I told him I knew he killed his family."

"How do you know that?"

"Because, sir, I was there."

THIRTY THREE

The Saranac Lake police contacted the Keene Police Chief, Mark Winston, about the statements made by Milton Brownfield. Winston did not seem to be surprised and said he would be over within the next forty-five minutes.

"Let him know I'm on my way."

"He wants to leave."

"Do everything you can to detain him."

"Well, we'll try our best. See you in a little while."

Winston realized his more important task was to discover the whereabouts of Todd Wilford. Was he a murderer? Did he really kill his mother, father and sister? And could he have possibly panicked and pushed his grandmother, Mary Metcalf, into the ravine by the covered bridge in Jay? If he was the murderer he seemed pretty calm up until now. Perhaps the pressure was taking an effect on him. Winston's concern was Todd might be capable of doing anything.

Something was missing. It just did not seem to make any sense. He thought to himself what reasons would Todd Wilford have to murder his family? Winston was somewhat overwhelmed by all of the occurrences. He decided to contact his best friend and trustworthy colleague, Jason Euling.

THIRTY FOUR

"I haven't heard from you in a while."

"Well, that's my fault."

"Tell me what's going on down there. I've been reading the updates on the Wilford case by looking at the internet accounts."

"Well, that's not even the whole story. I'm sure you know that's why I'm calling."

Mark Winston knew he could always count on his friend and closest confidant, Jason Euling, to assist him and provide possible suggestions and ideas to guide him with another baffling case. Winston always expected to live a quiet and peaceful life as the police chief of Keene. But that did not seem to be a reality.

"As you know George and Janet Wilford along with their daughter, Sabrina, were tied up in their home and gagged. The daughter died from smoke inhalation. The parents each suffered fatal gun wounds. And as you know, the house was set on fire."

"Mark, I am sure you know the published reports are speculating in many different directions. And I know you are dealing with two other deaths along with Edgar Metcalf's odd reappearance."

Winston replied,

"Edgar coming back set off a lot of dissension and confusion."

He paused and then continued, "The death, and possible horrific murder of Mary Metcalf truly has made things complicated."

"Mark, let me put my thoughts together. I'll see you in a couple of days, if not sooner."

"Jason, thank you."

"You are welcome."

THIRTY FIVE

Todd was able to blend in well at the campgrounds in the town of Wilmington. He had abandoned Sean's car in Saranac Lake and was able to make his way to Wilmington. He had been able to pitch a tent in the woods on the outer edge of the campgrounds by the lake. He felt bad but he stole a tent from the sporting goods store down the road. But he also knew his time was limited as to how long he could hide out at this location.

The second night a couple of people engaged Todd in a conversation. Out of curiosity they asked Todd where he was from. They also said they were impressed by his primitive fishing skills and the number of fish he was able to catch.

Todd did his best to remain calm as he did not want to appear a bit nervous. He was able to conclude their conversation without drawing any suspicion on their part. Todd then knew he had to be on the move.

He also needed to prove to someone, anyone who would listen, that he did not murder his family. Milton could not help him. In fact, he was trying to implicate him. Edgar was dead. And so was his aunt, Mary Metcalf. He knew he had to contact Sean. But he knew he would probably be upset with him for taking his car.

Todd's cell phone began to ring. The call, believe it or not, was from Sean.

"Hello."

"Todd, where are you?!"

"Sean, I'm sorry about your car."

"Todd, are you safe?"

"Yes."

"Where are you?"

"I can't tell you."

"Todd, let me help you. Trust me."

"Sean, I know everybody thinks I did this."

108

"Todd, listen to me. You need to come back to my house."

"I can't."

"Todd, I can help you."

"What? How can you help me? No one can."

"Todd, Edgar's wife, Patricia, is at my house. She is waiting to see you. Believe me she is shattered by Edgar's death. And now she is worried about you."

Sean paused for a few moments. He knew Todd was silent on the other end but he knew he had to wait out Todd on this.

"Are you still there Sean?"

"Yes."

"Why does she want to see me?"

"She says she has something to tell you. She said it is very important." Then the phone went dead.

THIRTY SIX

"A champion is a dreamer that refuses to give up."

Patricia Metcalf came to Sean's house a couple of hours ago. Along with her was Police Chief Winston. Sean's father, Ryan, and Sean's uncle, Michael, had also come to Sean's house.

"Patricia, please tell us what our father told you."

Patricia looked frightened and exhausted at the same time. Edgar's death and the circumstances of his situation were rather overwhelming. Sean offered Patricia a cup of tea. She welcomed it.

"Patricia, I know it has been a whirlwind for you," said Ryan.

Ryan was bewildered by Edgar's disappearance so many years ago. And then suddenly came back to Keene! Ryan continued, "I know you must be overwhelmed but it seems as if you want to tell us something."

Patricia sipped from her tea, which was still steaming. She began to speak slowly in a deliberate manner, "I'm not trying to be difficult." She paused for a few moments. "I am so shattered. My daughters are worried I'll get depressed. But right now I feel I need to tell you something."

She again hesitated. She was gazing out at the beautiful view of Hurricane Mountain. She then looked straight at Ryan and said, "I believe my husband murdered the Wilfords."

THIRTY SEVEN

Just as Patricia shocked everybody in the room with her thoughts about Edgar, there was a knock at the front door. Sean got up, opened the front door and standing before them was Todd Wilford.

"Todd, are you alright?"

"Yeah…I think so."

"Come in."

Todd walked in. Patricia got up and gave Todd a hug and a kiss on the cheek.

"Todd, are you okay?"

"Yes. What about you?"

"Well, Todd, all these people care about us."

"I know that."

"Where did you go?"

Todd looked over to Sean.

"Sean, I'm real sorry about your car."

"Todd, don't worry. You are here now. That's all that counts."

Chief Winston became somewhat uncomfortable, especially with Patricia Metcalf's statements about her husband, Edgar Metcalf and the sudden reappearance of Todd Wilford.

"Excuse me…" said Winston, "I need to step outside for a few minutes."

As Winston did so, the Metcalf family began to ask Todd questions.

"Were you at your house when the fire started?" asked Michael Metcalf, Ryan's brother.

"Yes."

"Were you alone?"

"No."

Todd continued to give details to all of them.

"Jason, this is Mark."

Jason listened to Mark as he gave an account of the latest occurrences.

"Jason, can you meet me at my house?"

"Yes, I'm assuming you found out some new revelations."

"Yes, I know Patricia Metcalf believes Edgar murdered the Wilford family. But that can't be true."

"Let's talk when I get to your house."

THIRTY EIGHT

The Police Chief came back into Sean's house.

"Is everything alright?" said Ryan

"Folks, I need to leave. Something has come up I have to take care of. Ryan, I'll call you later."

"Okay. Be safe."

Winston left the house. The weather was spectacular. It was a nice, cool autumn day. He only wished his mood could match the weather.

When he pulled up to his house Jason Euling had already arrived. Mark got out of his car and Jason came up to him and gave him a warm embrace. These two men almost looked identical. They were of the same height, weight and build. They both looked younger than their ages as they both kept themselves in great shape. When seen together, they were often mistaken to be brothers. Some even thought they were twins.

"Jason, it's great to see you."

"You too buddy."

The two of them walked inside the gorgeous cabin. Mark's family was away at his in-law's home at the Jersey shore. Mark was hoping to meet them there this weekend, but that did not look too hopeful at this time.

They sat down at the dining room table. Jason had a file folder with him and also took out his iPhone. He brought up an image of a person on the screen and showed it to Mark.

"This is who murdered the Wilford family."

"That is not possible!"

"Mark, it is. Let me explain."

THIRTY NINE

"I know it will not make sense, but she was there when the fire occurred. I do not know how yet, but she was."

"I don't understand. She has been confined. In fact, there is no way she could be released!"

"But, Mark, rumor has it that she has been hiding out at Crown Point."

"What do you mean? How could that be possible?"

"It's possible. There are some real remote areas at the Crown Point Historic Site."

"Do you think Ryan and Rita Metcalf know that Ryan's sister is back in the area? Why wouldn't the institution director notify them if she had left again?"

"I doubt if the Metcalfs know at this time. I'm sure she will make contact with one of them. She was supposed to be returning to the place up in Canada. But if she is in this area, as I believe she is, she could be very dangerous."

Mark had no reason to doubt Jason's discoveries. He has always been reliable with information and findings in the past. But how could she be the person who committed such a horrific crime, by herself no less?

FORTY

Jason Euling was well educated about all of the sensational murder cases of the Adirondacks. His knowledge of the alleged North Country wife killer, Henry DeBosnys, was astounding. Jason was often invited to give presentations on the 1882 murder case.

Henry DeBosnys was a stranger to many. In fact, many people found the circumstances of the case to be rather peculiar. From the time Henry DeBosnys came on the scene in Essex village in May 1882 and until August 1882, when his wife's body was discovered in the woods, his behavior was bizarre at best.

Jason Euling could recite the details of the case verbatim. He never needed to refer to notes or resources whenever he discussed the murder case. Mark Winston was also enthralled by the way Jason could captivate the audience, no matter how big or small.

Henry DeBosnys married his wife, Betsey Wells, after only courting her for four weeks. Betsey was previously married, was a respectable widow, and had four daughters. She owned a farm of fifteen acres. Her marriage to DeBosnys was followed by frequent spats caused by her refusal to give him rights to her property.

Betsey Wells' body was found in a hollow, covered with leaves. There were two pistol shots in her head and a gash to the neck straight through her spine.

This was just one of many murder cases Jason Euling had an incredible talent to recall such distinct details. Thus Mark Winston needed Jason Euling's skill with discovering who murdered the Wilford family. What Winston found unbelievable was that some of the details of the DeBosnys case were similar to the Wilford murders. What was going on?

FORTY ONE

She began to speculate to herself and talk to herself out loud.

"I know they'll never discover my whereabouts here at Crown Point.

"They have pretty much forgotten about me."

She was overlooking the grounds of the Crown Point reservation. Remarkably she had been able to hide out at this site for quite a long time. She disguised herself by volunteering at the site but also finding places to sleep at night whether it was at the historical officers' barracks, which had been covered for protection, or by setting a tent up in the remote area of the site. Sometimes, she would get inside the museum facility to protect herself from the harsh elements of the winter.

She continued to talk out loud,

"I know my father, Edgar, is my only real obstacle. He is such an odd man. Why would he come back to Keene now after abandoning us so long ago?"

A noise startled her. A groundskeeper was doing his rounds. He spotted her.

"Hey, what are you doing here?"

But she was able to conceal herself. The groundskeeper could not find her anywhere even though he searched for her for almost a full hour. She never had this problem before, even when she ventured to Keene to see her family and then come back to Crown Point. She was always able to keep herself concealed.

FORTY TWO

"To get what you want, stop doing what isn't working."

Mark and Jason sat down together and began to compare their thoughts on the Wilford murder case. There were many rumors. But Jason knew Mark was looking to him to act as a third party to sort out the case as it had presented itself. There was no good reason to get caught up in the small town gossip and rumor mongering; it was a complete waste of time to do so.

"I have no doubt this is a triple homicide along with a case of arson."

"I know that Jason," Mark responded in a quick manner. It was obvious the stress of the case was taking a toll on him. And he knew Jason was not offended by his quick response.

"Mark, there are different suspects. But let's eliminate who we can."

"I agree. Can we discuss Todd Wilford first?"

Jason stated, "There's no possibility he murdered his family. But he may have seen who did."

"How could that be?"

"First, he lived through this horrific event. Second, he has no past history to do such a misdeed. Third, he hinted as to who was in the area."

"Who did he mention? I was not aware of that."

"I firmly believe there was more than one person involved. One is a male and the other is a female. And, Mark, Edgar Metcalf is not the male."

"If not him, then who could have done this?"

"I will get to that. Retrieve your notes from the computer. I'll show you."

FORTY THREE

Josephine Metcalf was a very troubled
young lady. She was institutionalized at a
very young age. Her parents, Edgar and
Mary, had made a very difficult decision to
place Josephine in an institution. The
doctors guided the Metcalfs on the bizarre
behaviors their daughter would exhibit and
that as she got older, she would not be able
to function as a productive individual in
every day society. The doctors expressed
Josephine had a very rare gene that develops
into a person misbehaving in a very violent
manner. Only a constricted environment
with the proper monitoring of medication
could provide a stable life for Josephine.

But now it seemed as if Josephine had not
been living at the Canadian institution for
quite some time. The Metcalfs had been
notified but her whereabouts had been
unknown until now. Was she in Keene? Was
she really at the Wilford house the day of

the fire? Was she seen in the area? Was she with anyone else? There were just too many questions swirling around in Mark's head; this was more the reason he needed Jason's expertise. Mark was unable to think rationally.

Josephine Metcalf wanted her family to know she could outmaneuver them. She was more intelligent than any of them gave her credit. She had worked in mysterious ways that her family never suspected her of doing. And she was convinced they would never know she was at the Wilford house when the fire occurred. Only her friend knew. But she wondered how her father, Edgar, could possibly know.

She decided to make her way to Keene by herself. Her mode of transportation was a moped she kept hidden at the Crown Point Historic Site.

FORTY FOUR

"Jason, I trust you on this. What is our next step?"

Jason looked at Mark in an intense manner, knowing what he would say would affect the fabric of the entire community of Keene and the surrounding area.

"Mark, we need to meet with Ryan Metcalf and his family. They will be both devastated and yet not really surprised to hear that Ryan's sister masterminded the murders of George, Janet and Sabrina Wilford."

Mark got up from his chair, walked over to the telephone in his office and placed a call to the Metcalf household. The phone rang, what seemed like, incessantly. No one picked up and oddly enough, the answering machine was not operating.

Mark hung up the telephone, looked at Jason and simply said,

"Something is wrong Jason.

"She's there. I had a bad feeling about this," said Mark in a dismayed manner.

FORTY FIVE

Jason asked Mark to let him drive so he could theorize even more so about what was happening. As they departed to go to the Metcalf house, Jason began to explain to Mark what he believed occurred and how there was more than one person responsible for the horrific murders.

"Josephine Metcalf is a very astute woman. She is trying to sensationalize this case similar to the wife killer Henry DeBosnys' 1882 murder mystery."

"How do you know that?"

"Josephine has become a prime suspect in a series of unresolved missing person cases, as was Henry DeBosnys. She kept a journal that was discovered by the Crown Point groundskeeper. DeBosnys did likewise by scribing poetry."

"Have you seen Josephine's journal?"

"Yes, I read it. It is rather detailed. She names particular names. You will recognize most if not all of them. She never incriminates herself. She has different lists of people. She also describes the Wilford murder scene in detail."

"What names?"

"Her own family members she wrote about in her journal. She has a plan."

"Do you think she is at her family's house right now?"

"Yes. It is stated in her journal. We need to get there."

FORTY SIX

Josephine rode along the main road on her moped. She knew the family would be expecting her. Ryan, her brother, is known to be an outstanding detective so she knew they would not be surprised when she arrived. Her whereabouts were no longer secretive. She wanted to see her family's bewilderment when she appeared in front of them. If only that Crown Point groundskeeper had not spotted her. She could have remained in obscurity.

As she drove up the driveway to her family's home, she began to feel a sense of calm. The shock for all of them would feel absolutely invigorating to her. For so long she knew her family acted as if she did not exist. Over the years she kept track of her mother, father and two brothers. But she also always knew of the whereabouts of her supposedly dead father, Edgar Metcalf.

"Ryan, someone is coming up the driveway."

Ryan looked out the front window. Before he did so, he already knew who the visitor would be.

"Rita, honey, I know who it is."

"Who is it?"

"My sister is back."

Rita just stood in silence then sat down. She dreaded this day ever coming. She had turned rather pale. Then there was a rather sharp knock at the front door. Even though Rita expected it, she still shuddered. Why was Josephine here? This, on top of Edgar's return just seemed so overwhelming.

Again, the person knocked.

"I'm coming."

Ryan opened the door. The young lady looked remarkably like her mother, Mary.

"Josephine, please come in."

She hugged her brother. As she did so, Rita stood up from the couch and walked over to her sister-in-law and said,

"I'm glad you're here."

Josephine, looked at Rita, began to laugh out loud and simply said,

"Yeah, right."

FORTY SEVEN

"Do you know why I'm here? Do you even care?"

Sean came into the room. He seemed calm, especially with such odd circumstances.

"Hello Sean. I bet you did not expect to see me. I'm your Aunt Josephine."

"I know who you are. And I know you've been staying at the Crown Point reservation. I've known for quite a while."

"What, Sean, why didn't you say something?" exclaimed his father.

"I also know you want us to think you had something to do with the murders of the Wilfords."

"Sean, what are you saying?" his mother said in an agitated manner.

The telephone began to ring. After the fourth ring, the answering machine came on and the message could be heard by everyone in the room.

"Ryan. It's Jason Euling. Give me a call as soon as you are able to do so. I have news of interest for you."

Josephine looked at her brother. She seemed somewhat agitated upon hearing Jason Euling's voice. She began to perspire.

"I want all of you to sit down right now. I have some questions."

"Josephine, we are your family. Please slow down and tell us what is going on," her mother said in a calm manner.

Suddenly Josephine exploded, "My family!?! All of you put me away. You have had nothing to do with me. You didn't even look for me when I left the institution." Josephine could hardly contain herself. Her family was becoming anxious; they realized Josephine was not taking her medications to control her behavior. She was getting louder and louder. She almost seemed to be out of control. Ryan slowly began to walk toward Josephine.

"Ryan, don't come any closer! I have a gun!"

"Josephine, we are here to help you."

"How could any of you possibly help me!?"

"Josephine," said Sean, "Please tell us what is going on."

She backed up a few steps. The front door behind her began to open but she did not take notice. Standing in the doorway was Jason Euling.

"Josephine, it is over," said Jason. Josephine turned around to see who was behind her, slipped and hit the back of her head on the stone floor.

"Ryan, call for an ambulance. She is not breathing!"

Ryan did so.

Jason also said, "Josephine did not murder the Wilfords but she was outside the house when the fire started. She knows who committed the murders."

The ambulance arrived within ten minutes. But it was too late as Josephine had suffered a massive heart attack.

FORTY EIGHT

**"Excellence is doing ordinary things
extraordinarily well."**

Police Chief Mark Winston had called the
Metcalfs, Ryan and Rita, to meet him at his
office in Keene. Everything had become so
complicated with the reappearances of
Ryan's father, Edgar Metcalf, and Ryan and
Michael's sister, Josephine Metcalf. And
now with the sudden death of Josephine,
oddly enough, many loose ends were about
to be tied up. That is why Winston asked
Ryan and Rita to meet with him.

The autumn colors were brilliant, in an
almost festive manner. But that did not
match the mood of the people of Keene.
Many of them felt stunned and relieved at
the same time. Upon Josephine's death, the
actual murderer had been arrested. This was

all due to a letter found in the jacket Josephine was wearing when she collapsed and died. Ryan and Rita were not aware of the letter or of its startling contents. Albeit the reason for Chief Winston to meet with Josephine's family.

FORTY NINE

"I know this is very difficult for both of you and your family. We have made an arrest of the person responsible for the murders of the Wilford family members. I am sorry for the loss of Josephine."

"Thank you, Mark. Everything has been so overwhelming. We appreciate all you have done for us."

Mark hesitated for a few moments. Then he proceeded,

"I need to give both of you something. It is a letter written by Josephine. I believe it will help both of you with the healing process."

Mark handed them a copy of the letter. The Metcalfs left his office, got in their car and drove to their favorite spot overlooking Hurricane Mountain. Rita opened the letter and began to read it out loud:

I have been in pain for a very long time. I realize why my parents sent me to the rehabilitation center in Canada. I know it was for my own general welfare and safety. But I also know it was to protect me from harming others. Yet I felt abandoned. My therapist often said I was going through the stages similar to the stages of death: shock, denial, anger, adaptation, and acceptance. Well, guess what....acceptance never has occurred. I knew I had to get out of the place.

And I did. If you are reading this letter that must mean I died. There is no way I would have provided this letter to anyone whatsoever. So you must have discovered it in the pocket of my jacket. See....I did not murder the Wilfords but I did have someone do so for me. I needed to show people I still could be in control.

I watched as the house got torched. You may think Todd Wilford murdered his family but you are wrong. He only got his friend to get the gasoline as Todd planned on using it for something else. And you see I know who committed the murders but should I let you know in this letter?

Rita paused for a few moments almost as if she needed to catch her breath. She looked over to Ryan. They both wondered what else Josephine wrote in the letter.

There was a loud noise behind them. It startled both of them. Suddenly standing before them was the person who murdered the Wilfords! How could it be?

FIFTY

"What are you doing here?"

"Don't give that smug look? You know exactly why I'm here. Do I really need to explain myself?!"

Both Rita and Ryan tried to keep themselves calm.

"Go ahead. Keep reading the letter. Don't you want to know what Josephine wrote?"

Ryan turned to him and said, "How do you know what's in this letter? I thought no one else saw it?"

"See that's your problem. It always has been. You are always questioning everything. Well, take your time reading the letter as it will be the last thing you'll ever do."

All three of them remained quiet for a few moments.

Suddenly he bellowed, "Read it! Now! I want to hear you read it Aunt Rita!"

Rita looked alarmed but then said, "I'm not your aunt. Don't refer to me as such. Do you hear me?"

The man did not respond so she began to read the letter where she left off.

Realize I am not the one directly responsible for the Wilford family murders. Todd may have been in the house but his buddy did the dirty work. Sad to say, Todd knew the fire was going to occur but he did not realize how brutal the murders of his family members would become. Todd expected to receive insurance money. By this time I am sure Todd is still awaiting the monies from the insurance company. Don't you think it was odd that Todd sustained little or no injuries from both the fire and leaping from the second floor window? Don't you think it is also odd that Todd was not harmed, tied up and gagged? Was it not odd that Todd escaped so easily and did not try to assist his parents and sister? I'm sure as you read this, especially you, Ryan Metcalf, how could you not question the authorities more about the status of the triple homicide and the fire?

By now I am sure you are wondering who the individual is who committed such a horrific crime!

FIFTY ONE

Chief Winston called Ryan Metcalf on his cell phone but there was no answer. He wanted to make sure Ryan and his wife, Rita, were okay after reading Josephine's letter. Winston knew they would never be the same but at least there would be some closure.

He tried to ring them a second time but decided then to leave a message.

"Ryan, it is Mark. Pick up if you are there. It's important."

Mark thought to himself he needs to contact Jason as soon as possible. Something didn't feel right. Ryan never lets the phone just ring once and go straight to voicemail, especially since he had told the Metcalfs he would be in touch within a reasonable time to check on them. He knew that Josephine's letter would be earth shattering, especially with the person she reveals as being the murderer.

Mark was not really taken back by who Josephine implicated, especially since Jason had given him a pre-warning as to what to expect.

Ryan could feel the cell phone vibrating in his pocket but did not want the man to become aware that he was receiving a phone call. He was glad he had put the phone on a vibrate mode earlier in the day. He speculated to himself as to who it could be; he figured it was either his son, Sean or Jason. He also knew if he checked the man would confiscate the phone.

The man repeated his demand.

"Read the rest of the letter. I want both of you to hear out loud every detail Josephine wrote. I want to see your faces when you hear the information Josephine wrote. You'll be surprised by the way she went about orchestrating such a gruesome crime. And how she manipulated me to do what I did."

Ryan just leered at the man.

"I said read it! Now!"

FIFTY TWO

Jason knew exactly what he needed to do. He knew where Rita and Ryan had gone to read the letter Mark Winston had given them. He knew where they could gain some peace while they read the contents of the letter. But he also knew time was of the essence as the killer was already there with them. How could anything get worse for the Metcalfs? Too many things had occurred for one family to endure. It was almost incredible to think that Mary Metcalf, Edgar Metcalf and now Josephine Metcalf were all dead. Jason knew he had to get to the summit where not only Rita and Ryan were at but so was the murderer.

The man continued to scream at Rita and Ryan.

"I don't really care how long it takes you to read the letter as you're not leaving here. Ever!"

There was some noise down the trail from where they were seated. The man became distracted. Rita and Ryan did not see anyone but the man began to shout out, "Who's there? I know someone is there!"

A thunderous gun shot went off. The man ducked. Both Rita and Ryan did the same as they took cover. The man was not moving. Then he got up. Another sound could be heard down the trail. The man went over to Rita and Ryan and had them sit back to back. He then tied and gagged them. The man then said he would be back. He ran down the trail. He was pretty agile for a big man. He got down to the bottom of the trail within fifteen minutes. His car was at the same spot he had left it, hidden among the trees. No one should be able to notice his vehicle but as he approached it, he was alarmed to see that his passenger front door was ajar.

He heard a noise behind him.

"So I guess you did not expect to see me. Get your hands up in the air. Now it's my turn to end this ordeal," he said in a calm manner.

FIFTY THREE

The two men climbed back up the trail. The person who had been threatening the Metcalfs at the top of the trail did not seem so bold anymore. He had become somewhat reticent to even engage in a conversation with the individual who startled him when he noticed his car door was wide open.

"Move faster. I know you are not tired. You're an athlete. I know you are not winded. So move it!"

The weather was changing quickly. The Adirondacks often experienced fast weather changes. Both of these men realized that; the clouds were darkening and the wind was beginning to pick up. Neither one of them wanted to exhibit any type of anxiety. They both realized the weather could curtail them getting to the summit and confronting Rita and Ryan Metcalf. A flash in the sky caused both of them to jump. With that they both scattered in different directions as it became extremely dark in an eerie sort of way.

"Stop! Come back here!" But there was no response. He knew he had to find him or the entire plan would blow up. No one could ever find out he murdered the Wilfords. And that he was in the area when Mary Metcalf fell into the stream by the covered bridge in Jay. No one!

FIFTY FOUR

"The best way to predict the future is to invent it."

A rustling could be heard down the trail. The Metcalfs had been able to remove the rope binding their wrists. They knew they would either have to hide or act as if they had not been able to rid themselves of the rope that had been used to tie them up back to back. Amazingly the sky had cleared up in dramatic fashion, though the temperature had dropped by about eight to ten degrees. Ryan and Rita were anxious to continue reading Josephine's letter. A man came running up from the path. It was not Todd. Rita and Ryan could hardly believe who was standing before them. They also realized that Josephine would identify that same person in her letter.

Ryan simply said, "How could you have done such a thing? The Wilfords were always kind to you. And now you intend to carry out your plan."

The man cleared his throat before he responded, "What do you mean? How do you know about my plan?"

"I read the rest of Josephine's letter. Let me read it to you."

"Not now."

"Yes, now. You need to hear this," said Ryan.

Rita began to read the letter out loud by repeating the last sentence she had already read,

But now I am sure you are wondering who could commit such a horrific crime? Well, don't be surprised. He probably has tried to blackmail Todd. He has probably convinced the legal authorities that he was too weak to commit such horrible murders. He probably manipulated the Wilfords so they would trust him. And if I am correct, he is probably right before you as he tries to again deflect any suspicion upon him. He is slick. He thinks he can fool everybody. Now I know you think I may not have him figured out, but I do. He tried to get Todd to murder his own family. But Todd relented yet got caught up in what he was trying to do. His plan was to murder the Wilfords and pin the murder on Todd.

"That's enough. I'm not listening to anymore of this. Get up. We're going down the trail."

Rita and Ryan Metcalf rose slowly. They realized he could end their lives at any moment. He seemed somewhat out of control. He was practically stumbling over his feet. He almost looked like he was drunk. The pressure was getting to him.

"I said get up and start down the trail!"

"You're not going to get away with this," said Rita.

"Just keep walking!"

FIFTY FIVE

Police Chief Mark Winston along with Jason Euling made their way up the trail with ten other officers from surrounding towns. This had become quite an ordeal as the group had received contact from Ryan Metcalf. They were informed that the killer is armed and dangerous. Jason had gotten word from Ryan by receiving a terse text message, but it was both precise and alarming. Jason knew all along in his heart that Todd Wilford had not committed these murders but there was concern that he could be considered an accomplice. Todd, though, had been cooperating with the authorities to help capture the real killer.

"Jason, you do not seem surprised by who the prime suspect is."

"No. It wasn't obvious at first, but he has been patterning the notorious wife murderer, Henry DeBosnys."

Mark had heard Jason tell the story of Henry DeBosnys numerous times, yet he never was bored by the tale Jason spoke of. Mark found it fascinating and always came away with learning something else new about the murderer. And now that Jason firmly felt there were parallels to the Wilford murders made it more compelling.

And sure enough, Jason spoke about a part of the case he had not heard about.

Henry DeBosnys was rather ill when he was arraigned. He looked like a sickly individual. He had been treated with mercury to combat his illness. Oddly enough Sabrina Wilford's body contained arsenic when the autopsy was completed. DeBosnys had experienced uncontrollable drooling. In 1883, people were not aware of the side effects mercury could cause. DeBosnys also speculated that he been set up. He claimed he did not murder his wife. The murderer of the Wilford family has also renounced his innocence. He continually tries to pass on the suspicion to other individuals, particularly to Todd Wilford. DeBosnys claimed that evidence was planted to look as if he was the killer. And the murderer of the Wilfords has stated that Todd Wilford retrieved the gas container and started the fire at the Wilford home. Oddly enough too, Henry DeBosnys had also been known by another name of Keff. Josephine Metcalf also had used another name to hide her identity so people would not connect her to the Metcalf family.

"Jason, could I ask you a question?"

"Sure."

"What does this have to do with the Wilford case?"

"Don't you see? It's simple. The murderer is…"

A loud boom was heard. What could have made such an enormous sound? Jason, Mark and the crew began to run along the trail toward the noise.

FIFTY SIX

The explosive had detonated in his hand. The pain was excruciating. But even so, he could still aim his gun at the Metcalfs and warned them not to move. He was losing blood quickly and was becoming lightheaded. He needed to escape from this situation as soon as possible. He knew Chief Winston was probably on his way along with that mastermind, Jason Euling.

"Get up and come this way! We're going up farther on this trail to the summit."

The blood was dripping down his arm. He knew it would only be a matter of time before he would lose sense of what to do next. He also had a deep wound in his abdomen as a piece of the explosive lodged itself above his waist. He did not think the Metcalfs knew. But then the blood was seeping out of his jacket.

"Listen, I know you are hurt bad. I can help you."

"Why?"

"You need assistance or you're going to die," said Ryan. "Let me help you."

"Fine," the young man said weakly.

"Let me look at your hand. Wow. You're bleeding real badly from your stomach.'

"I know that." His legs began to buckle. He dropped the gun and it went off. The bullet ricocheted off a rock in the distance. No one was harmed by it. Rita took some bandages out of the backpack she had carried with her. She also had some first aid ointment but when she looked at the wounds, she nodded to Ryan in a manner that signaled there was no hope for the man. The man passed out and his breathing became rather shallow. Ryan and Rita tried to make him comfortable as they both knew it would only be a matter of time before the man died.

Behind them Ryan and Rita could hear people coming up the trail. They both knew it would be Chief Winston and Jason. They appeared within moments.

With that Jason walked over to Ryan, put his hand on his shoulder, and said, "You found him. The murderer of the Wilford family is dead."

FIFTY SEVEN

The service for the murderer was about to begin. The oddity was that it would be held in the Keene Town Hall. The local minister decided to not allow the funeral to occur at his church. He felt it would be inappropriate for such a thing to occur as the killer was not religious and the situation was beyond comprehension. He knew the good Lord might disagree but he was at peace with his decision.

The gathered crowd was rather subdued. They wondered who would deliver the eulogy when to the amazement of practically everybody, Todd Wilford made his way across the stage and stood at the podium.

He began by saying,

"Good morning. To be candid, I am sure you did not expect me to be the individual to deliver a speech on behalf of the deceased. I am the only living relative willing to do so.

And for your information, after this service concludes, I will be taken into custody by the authorities.

So please let us begin with a prayer from Psalm 62:

In God alone be at rest, my soul,

For my hope is from him.

He alone is my rock, my salvation.

My fortress; never shall I falter."

Todd paused for what seemed like an enormous amount of time. Then he continued,

"In God is my salvation and glory,

My rock of strength;

In God is my refuge.

Trust him at all times. O people,

Pour out your hearts before him, for God is our refuge."

Todd paused again, bowed his head for a few moments, then looked up at the assembled people and began to speak softly.

"See, my cousin did not plan to murder my family. Things got out of control. Josephine Metcalf had convinced him that the Wilfords were to blame for her institutionalization. My Dad, George Wilford, had prepared legal documents for Josephine's brother and sister-in-law, Ryan and Rita Metcalf to sign and authorize. Josephine had convinced my cousin that revenge was the only way to seek condemnation. My cousin always knew Josephine had kept herself hidden at the Crown Point Historic Site. But it wasn't until the night of the fire he told me of his and Josephine's plan to torch my house. But he panicked and killed my parents He did this after he had placed me in an adjoining room. He had gagged me and tied my hands behind my back and bound my ankles."

There were gasps from many different people in the audience. Police Chief Winston was concerned with the atmosphere of the assembly. But what could he do to cease Todd's speech.

"I am saddened by what has happened. During the last few weeks it has been harrowing for so many of us. My parents and sister being murdered has been excruciating…."

171

Todd had a difficult time holding back tears but after a few moments he was able to continue.

"The losses of Mary Metcalf, Edgar Metcalf and Josephine Metcalf have been absolutely astounding. Why do we keep suffering so much in our small town of Keene? We need to stick together as one."

Now Chief Winston was noting how the assembly was becoming somewhat restless. He had never experienced such a thing. Todd was working the crowd the same way Edgar Metcalf had done so many years ago. But the people were anxious with Todd's approach. Many faulted him for the deaths of his family members.

Todd then said, "Even though he is no longer with us we must forgive Milton Brownfield for his actions."

Suddenly a man from the back of the town hall spoke up and said, "Not so fast son. You need to deal with reality. Josephine tried to protect you. Let me tell the real story."

Todd could only leer at Jason Euling. Todd suddenly was at a loss as to what he should do next.

"I suggest you come with me. It is in your best interest to do so."

Todd could only leer at Jason balling. Todd
suddenly was at a loss as to what he should
do next.

"I suggest you come with me. It is in your
best interest to do so."

FIFTY EIGHT

Todd Wilford walked up to the front porch of Ryan and Rita's house. He was escorted by Ryan and Rita's son, Sean. Pulling up in a Dodge pickup truck were Jason Euling and Police Chief Mark Winston. Already inside was Patricia Metcalf. It was quite a cast of characters. In addition, the mayor of Keene, Joan Galente, was invited to the meeting. Todd realized Jason Euling's association with Mark Winston made this situation very imposing. He also was well aware that Milton Brownfield had been apprehended for the murders of his mother, father and sister. Todd wondered what Jason Euling would reveal that he was not already aware of.

"Please let's have everyone sit down. I appreciate all of you being here," said Jason.

Todd wondered who was in charge of the meeting. With that thought, Mark Winston

175

stood up and began to direct his comments to Todd,

"First, Todd, please accept our deep sympathy for your loss."

"Thank you, sir."

"Second, Todd, I must candidly tell you that I am somewhat disappointed by how you have been handling everything. I will say to you that you have acted quite immaturely and carelessly these past few weeks. I'm not sure why you associated with Milton Brownfield but I'll get to that in a few minutes."

Rita Metcalf walked in from the kitchen with coffee, cookies and a homemade pie. She asked everyone to help themselves. They did so. This seemed to break some of the tension in the room. Once everyone got settled back in their seats in the living room, Mark asked for Jason to continue with the discussion. Jason remained seated and then began to talk.

"Todd, you are very lucky to have all of these people with you today. They care about you and want to help you. But as Chief Winston mentioned, you have acted rather oddly. In fact, I am sure you know,

176

many think you had something to do with the murders of your family."

"I didn't sir."

"Let me continue. You need to listen carefully to everything I am about to tell you. Do you understand?"

"Yes sir." Sean was seated next to Todd. Todd always seemed to gain comfort from Sean as Sean was always level headed. Todd also knew Sean had endured his own legal predicament a short time ago.

"Todd, Josephine Metcalf may have meant to lure you into her plan of revenge. But you may have been somewhat naïve to realize the depth of her manipulation. As I am sure you are aware of by now, she wrote a rather detailed letter implicating different individuals."

"Am I one of them?" asked Todd anxiously.

"Let me take you through the account she left. You may not realize what harm she left behind."

FIFTY NINE

Jason realized he would have to go through quite a bit of detail to help not only Todd, but everyone seated in the room. As usual, he knew he had the full confidence of Mark Winston. He had informed Mark of his findings prior to this gathering. Jason wanted to be at the town hall, knowing that more than likely Todd would make false statements. Jason also knew Todd was not completely upfront with his statements to the legal authorities. Todd knew that Jason was about to reveal all of the details. Even though Todd, himself, knew he was not guilty of the horrific acts of murder and arson, he was still wary of what Jason was about to tell everybody.

"Josephine was a very sly young lady. As much as she had been placed in a rehabilitation center, she still had the mind of a very sophisticated individual, even though her mindset was criminal. She recruited Milton Brownfield to murder Todd's family. The original plan was to murder all four of them, including Todd, but Milton Brownfield did not, and could not carry out the entire scheme. In fact, for Todd's sake, he panicked when he realized he was about to murder his so called best friend, Todd."

There was absolute silence in the room. Each and every person waited for Jason to continue.

"See, Milton did ask Todd to retrieve a gas container. Milton also blindfolded and gagged Todd. Milton then went about committing the murders of the Wilford family. He was instructed by Josephine to kill Todd last so Todd could hear the excruciating deaths his family members would endure. As you can imagine it was harrowing. But see Milton never tied up Todd's ankles. He had led Todd to another room and as the flames became more ferocious and Todd began to scream for help, Milton pushed Todd out the window and he, himself, ran out the back door and off into the woods. The firemen and emergency personnel did not see Milton run down the trail behind the house. Nor did anyone see Josephine off to the side. She was not only there but she took a series of photographs on a cell phone. Amazingly, and fortunately for us, the cell phone was in the same coat pocket that contained the letter Josephine had on her when she died."

Todd was mesmerized by the account Jason was providing everybody. Still no one spoke or made any type of inquiries. Jason stopped for a few moments and took a sip of the ice water from the glass Rita provided him earlier.

Jason then said, "But there is more to the story. There are some concerns and items of interest I have been able to thoroughly research. But first I must speak to Sean privately."

SIXTY

"Tough times never last, but tough people do."

Sean went and sat with Jason on the front porch. Everyone else remained inside the house. It was getting cool outside as the sun was setting. The fall weather in the Adirondacks could often take a quick change in temperatures. Such was the case now as it was much colder outside than what it was when they first arrived at the Metcalf's house.

"Sean, you are probably Todd's closest ally. I need to ask you a few questions."

Sean seemed a little uncomfortable but then said, "Okay, whatever you need."

Jason proceeded to speak with Sean for almost twenty minutes.

"I want you to understand if it wasn't for your communication with Todd to return

183

home, this could have been even more complicated or actually fatal. Todd believed he was being hunted down and suspected as the murderer. You were able to provide him a safe haven"

"Thank you."

"But you also need to know that Todd's sister was also going to have a baby. She aborted the baby but the father did not know Sabrina had aborted the child. The father, Milton Brownfield, was convinced by Josephine that the only way to rid him having the burden of a child was to kill the Wilfords, torch the house and thus get rid of the evidence. Or so he thought."

Sean was overwhelmed by what Jason was telling him.

"I firmly feel Milton did not murder Todd as well as he suddenly realized how bizarre the entire situation had become. Josephine had masterminded a stunning plan and was able to somewhat brainwash Milton."

Sean began to feel light headed and then asked Jason, "Are my parents aware of all of this?"

"Your Dad is. He planned on telling your Mom and I am sure he did so already."

"Josephine was my aunt. I did not know her as my parents rarely ever made mention of her."

"Are you okay?"

"Yes."

"Okay. Let's go back inside."

SIXTY ONE

Jason and Sean walked back into the house. Rita walked over to her son, Sean, and gave him a hug. Todd looked confused.

Jason then spoke first, "Let me tell you where we are with the case."

Even though Ryan and Rita knew most of what Jason would tell them, they were very attentive. Patricia Metcalf did though look somewhat apprehensive. She was concerned and fearful that her deceased husband, Edgar, may have had a hand in the murders. But it did not seem as though Jason was alluding to Edgar Metcalf having something to do with the horrific crime.

"So let me continue. Milton Brownfield, if he was still alive, would be charged with murders of the Wilford family. In addition, arson would also be a charge. Josephine was definitely an accomplice to the murders. She masterminded this entire horrific scheme."

He paused for a few moments. Jason then said in a slow and deliberate manner, "There is also the death of Mary Metcalf. Mary's death was not accidental. Milton Brownfield was at the covered bridge at Jay as Mary sought solace there. As she was lost in thought, it has been accounted by two witnesses that Mary was pushed into the stream by Milton. Mary hit her head and was killed instantly. Ryan, Rita and Sean, I am truly sorry for your loss. And Ryan, please extend my condolences to your brother, Michael."

Everyone looked absolutely grief stricken. Jason knew his summary would be both painful and gut wrenching. But he knew he needed to provide each of them with all of the details.

"I must say I did have my concern that Edgar may have been in cohorts with Josephine but that was only a fleeting thought. Please understand my trepidation, Patricia, as his past would truly warrant great concern. But I do want to relieve you of what you may be thinking. Your husband did not have anything to do with murders of George, Janet and Sabrina Wilford. Nor was he involved in the death of Mary."

"Jason, I thank you for your involvement with this case. I know Mark has total confidence in your abilities to investigate and solve difficult situations. God bless you," said Patricia.

Jason just nodded his head. He looked to Mark for any additional guidance. Jason felt as if he had dominated the conversation, but that was exactly what Mark wanted him to do. In Mark's eyes, Jason was brilliant. His skills to discover the details of a crime were first to none. Mark knew that from the time they both went to and graduated from the police academy. Amazingly these two men never became enemies as they were always neck to neck with whatever came their way.

"Thank you, Jason, for being so thorough with all of your findings. Todd, I must say, you have been through a harrowing experience. I know your life has changed dramatically."

"Sir I thank you for believing in me. The night of my family's deaths was absolutely horrendous. I knew it was too late to stop Milton from doing what he planned. He was manipulated by Josephine the same way he did to me."

Todd began to have a difficult time keeping his emotions to himself. Yet he seemed to need to say something else.

"Aunt Rita and Uncle Ryan I can never thank you enough for all you have done for me."

"No, Todd, not us. Sean was the one."

"I know. But you, too, were there for me,"

"And, Todd, you can stay with us. For as long as you need."

With that Todd got up and shook Jason's hand, thanked him and then turned to Chief Winston. "Sir, I know I acted on an impulse. But I was afraid no one would believe my story. I took off because of the fear no one would believe I was telling the truth."

"Son, do not worry. We know everything was planned and committed by both Milton and Josephine."

EPILOGUE

"The best things in life aren't things."

Five years have passed by since the Wilford family was murdered. It has been rather uneventful during the past five years. In fact, Police Chief Winston had just recently commented to the county coroner, James Boyler, that his job had almost become dull; but he did not mind that whatsoever. During the first part of his term here in Keene he had to deal with the bizarre escapades of a lawyer named Sidney Emerson. He was a prominent lawyer in the area. But he had swindled people of their money and had actually committed murder himself. Chief Winston also had to deal with an odd murder case of a young couple. Their bodies were discovered atop Wright Mountain. Emerson was able to defend the suspect, Paul Pipford, and had him found not guilty. And then five years ago the shocking murders of the Wilford family members and the death of Mary Metcalf mesmerized the community.

"Jane, I am going to go visit the library and pick out a book and then go home for lunch."

"Okay, chief. Take your time."

"Do you want me to bring you anything back when I return?"

"No, sir, I will take my break when you return."

"Okay. I should only be gone for about forty minutes."

— — — — —

Patricia Metcalf, Edgar's second wife, realized she had to depart from Keene. Her husband had always had something he was wrestling with throughout their marriage. Eventually Patricia was able to persuade Edgar to let her know what was consuming him with such anxiety. When he did so, she was not so much as overwhelmed as she was baffled. How could Edgar have abandoned such a loving family in Keene? His wife, Mary, was a rather faithful person who was left to raise what turned out to be three children, Ryan, Michael and Josephine. Ryan and Michael, in particular, were rather

192

angered by Edgar's reappearance. And his daughter, Josephine, had been institutionalized, escaped from the facility, hid at Crown Point and then devised a terrible scheme to murder the Wilford family members. As much as Patricia may have wanted to stay in Keene, her daughters convinced her to return to their Canadian hometown and be nearby her daughters and their families. She departed not much after the Wilford case was resolved by Jason Euling. Each Christmas she sent a Christmas card and letter to the Metcalf family. She always received a letter in return keeping her up to date on the happenings with the Metcalfs and the people of Keene.

_ _ _ _ _

"Honey, I'm home. I only have a few minutes."

Mark's wife called down to him to let him know that his lunch was in the refrigerator. He took it out and sat down to eat it. His wife came down into the kitchen, kissed him hello and then said goodbye as she was off to run a few errands and then head over to the Lake Placid movie house to ready the theater for its latest movie premier. Mark's wife had been the manager of the movie house for the past three years and enjoyed her job. Mark finished up his lunch and headed back to the police station.

– – – – –

Sean Metcalf moved away from Keene and relocated to a small town outside of Cleveland. His wife had received a lucrative offering to become a lead book editor for a small publisher. Sean and his wife were not looking to leave Keene but the opportunity felt like the right thing for them to go forward with. It did mean uprooting their young son and leaving Sean's close knit family behind. It was though an exciting time as they also found out that Sean's wife was pregnant with twins. It was a bittersweet time for all of them. Their new home was quite unique in the sense that they had a brand new log cabin awaiting them.

– – – – –

A gentleman walked into the police station. He looked rather harried. He called out to see if anyone was in the offices. The front desk was left unoccupied. That did seem odd as it was known that there was always someone on duty, whether it was an officer or the secretary. And the man who had arrived was well aware of that as he was a close friend of Mark Winston. Again he called out. Then a car came into the parking lot. The man went outside to greet Police Chief Winston.

"Sam, how are you?"

"I'm good. It's quiet. What can I do for you?"

"Well, I came by to report something. But when I went inside no one is around."

"Oh, no, Sam, I know Jane is here. Did you go inside?"

"Yes, Mark. There is no one here."

"Let me check. Jane. Jane, I'm back."

There was no response. The front door had been open. The telephone answering machine was blinking.

"Sam, let me check outside." He did so and then said, "Jane's car is here. Let me see if her pocketbook is at her desk."

Mark went back inside. He quickly came back out and said to Sam, "Jane's pocketbook is under her desk and the cup of tea on her desk is still pretty hot. She must have left for a minute." But Mark felt something was wrong. She never left the office unattended. She knew I would not be long. Mark did not want Sam to recognize his anxiety.

"Sam, did you need to see me about something? Come back inside."

"Yes. Mark. I'm concerned with..."

The cell phone on Jane's desk began to ring. It startled Mark as it was the ring tone to Jane's cell phone. He hesitated to pick it up but did so and said, "Hello."

"Do you know where she is?!" shouted the person on the other end of the line.

– – – – –

Rita and Ryan continued to do a great amount of volunteer work in the community. Rita had taken on the role of Keene historian. She often consulted with the Keene library director. They collaborated on a town centennial project. This was a great rallying project for the townspeople. Rita was surprised by the wealth of information she discovered. Ryan encouraged his wife to publish a book on the history of Keene and in particular, the odd occurrences that Keene had experienced. Such tales as to the different murders would surely draw great interest. Ryan continued to promote his private investigation work. His endeavors assisted Rita with her research. Even though they sorely missed their son, Sean and his wife and their grandson, they kept busy. Ryan's brother, Michael, was a frequent visitor to their home, particularly for Sunday dinner. Michael had never married though he had a love interest he had been dating the past six months. She was a local gal whom Michael had graduated with from high school. The last few Sundays of the month Michael had brought her to Ryan and Rita's house for dinner. Michael had often mentioned to his brother, Ryan, that it seemed very quiet around town, especially since the Wilford family murder case was resolved.

— — — — —

"You better listen to me very carefully. I know where Jane is. But you'll never find her."

With that the person slammed down the phone. Mark looked extremely stunned; Sam asked him if everything was okay. With that Mark got on his phone and made a call to the only person who could help him.

_ _ _ _ _

Todd Wilford had graduated from high school as an academic scholar. In addition, he excelled in three sports: soccer, basketball and baseball. Remarkably he shattered practically every school record Sean Metcalf had set during his high school career. This was a blessing in disguise as his athletic success led to him receiving numerous scholarship offers. He elected to accept a football scholarship to one of the Division One SUNY colleges. His physical size and his ability to move about so well as a quarterback made his decision simple to pick football as the sport he wanted to pursue. Getting away from Keene could only help him to get a fresh start. The deaths of his family members and the overwhelming circumstances had become a great burden. Sean had persuaded him to not stay in Keene. Without Sean's guidance, Todd may have never taken the next step to go away for college. Todd planned to earn a degree in business administration and minor in sports administration. While at school, he was treated as a celebrity but as time went on he was able to blend in with the college crowd and not have to continually answer questions about his family's murders. Ironically, another person to keep him grounded was Jason Euling. He kept in contact with Todd almost on a daily basis and attended practically every one of Todd's football games, no matter where they were scheduled to be played.

— — — — —

Mark rang Jason's cell phone. The phone was not answered by Jason so Mark left a simple message, "Jason, call me. It's important."

No sooner did Mark end his call to Jason the phone rang. He assumed it was Jason, "Jason, thank you for calling me back."

"It's not Jason. I've got your secretary. And she is never going to be found. I'm up in the

199

mountains with her now. And don't expect your buddy, Jason Euling, to be too helpful. He knows I'm unstoppable. What's the matter? You have nothing to say??!!"

Mark then uttered with great fury, "You'll never get away with this!!" But Mark knew his response was futile. The caller had already hung up in less than ten seconds. Mark's phone rang again. This time Mark looked at the screen of the cell phone. It registered as Jason's number. Mark quickly activated the call and said, "Jason, I'm glad it's you.'

"Guess what, it's not Jason. I have Jane and I have Jason's cell phone. Figure that one out." The phone again was abruptly hung up. Mark looked bewildered. He had an awful feeling that this was not going to have a good ending. Mark turned to Sam and said, "Things have gotten bad again."

— — — — —

The young man just smiled to himself. He was overlooking the trail to his favorite high peak. They'll never find Jane. And they'll wonder if Jason Euling is alive.

ACKNOWLEDGEMENTS

It is a fascinating process when you research and create a novel. So many people of the Adirondacks region have been both responsive and supportive.

They include:

Keene Library Director Marcy LeClair in Keene, NY

Wells Memorial Library Director Karen Rappaport in Jay, NY

Keene Valley Library Director Karen Glass in Keene Valley, NY

Elizabethtown Library Director Lora Langston in Elizabethtown, NY

Saranac Lake Free Library Director Pete Benson in Saranac Lake, NY

Michele Tucker, Saranac Lake Free Library Researcher

Lake Placid Library Director Bambi Pedu in Lake Placid, NY

Adirondack History Center Museum Director Diane O'Connor

Sarah and Marc Galvin, Bookstore Plus
Owners in Lake Placid, NY

Crown Point Historic Site Museum Staff

Niki Kourofsky, Adirondack Life Senior
Editor

Goff-Nelson Memorial Library Director Peg
Mauer in Tupper Lake, NY

Moose Maple Bookstore in Saranac Lake,
NY

The front cover photograph depicts the
horrific devastation a fire can cause. The
back cover photographs are of the
September 1999 Noonmark Mountain blaze
in the Adirondacks (These photographs were
inspired by my wife's uncle, Jimmy Boyle).
Fire is a tough thing for people to combat. As
fire does, life also presents us with many
challenges.

Family and friends have often asked, "When
is the next book coming out?" Well, here it
is! I thank each and every one of you for
your support, whether it was moral,
spiritual, or emotional. As we know all of
these are vital for success!

My writing endeavors have always had the support and guidance of my wife Maryann, She is truly my rock. Our children Colleen, Michael and Patrick, and daughter-in-law Brittney, to whom this book is dedicated, have always been interested in the progress of my writings.

Always remember that faith and hope are both essential when it comes to doing the impossible.

"Know who you are, and be it. Know what you want, and go out and get it!"

-Carroll Bryant

LIST OF CHARACTERS

William Cameron, Fire Chief

Mark Winston, Keene Police Chief

Edgar Metcalf, Reverend

Patricia Metcalf, Edgar's Second Wife

Katherine Metcalf, Patricia and Edgar's Twin Daughter

Kelly Metcalf, Patricia and Edgar's Twin Daughter

George Wilford, Victim

Janet Wilford, Victim

Sabrina Wilford, Victim

Todd Wilford, George and Janet's Son

James Boyler, Coroner

Selma Griffin, Coroner's Secretary

Rita Smithly, Newspaper Reporter

Mark Winston, Keene Police Chief

Ryan Metcalf, Edgar's Son

Michael Metcalf, Edgar's Son

Rita Metcalf, Ryan's Wife

Sean Metcalf, Rita and Ryan's Son; Edgar's
Grandson

Mary Metcalf, Edgar's First Wife

Milton Brownfield, Suspect

Jason Euling, Mark Winston's Colleague
and Best Friend

Josephine Metcalf, Edgar and Mary's
Daughter (Ryan's Sister)

Hank Manson, Wilford Family Counsel

Father Gibson

Eric Dolloy, Suspect

Donna Galente, Mayor of Keene

Officer Tedesco

Henry DeBosnys, Wife Murderer

Paul Pipford, Past Defendant

Sydney Emerson, Deceased Lawyer

SKETCH # 1:

ESSEX COUNTY AND JAY

Essex County is 1,823 square miles contained on 1,166,720 acres. Essex County is roughly the size of the state of Delaware. It is the second largest county in New York State (The largest county is Lawrence County). Some think the Adirondack Forest Preserve is a waste of good land. But "Forever Wilders" think the preserve should be untouchable, eternally free of the inroads of civilization. The New York State Legislature created the Adirondack Forest Preserve in 1885. In 1892 the Adirondacks was formed. The 1894 New York State Constitutional Convention added a clause: "Nor shall the timber thereon be sold, removed or destroyed."

The town of Jay is much more residential than ever before. There has been a decline of agriculture. There is a continual seasonal influx of tourists. The residents of Jay rely on outside facilities for health care and public safety. Most residents of Jay have lived in the town for at least five years. Approximately fifty percent of the residents have lived here for twenty or more years.

The people take great pride in the architecture of the town and well maintained landscape. Jay was formed in 1798 and named for John Jay, a New York State governor and later Chief Justice of the United States Supreme Court.

Most of Jay is located in the area of the East Branch of Ausable River. Many people of Jay have low income and in some cases lower levels of schooling. An old adage states, "You make it in the summer or you don't eat all winter." People realize that tourism is the meat and potatoes of the region. Tourism brings in sales tax and profit. Some feel it is a lousy way to make a living.

SKETCH # 2:

Saranac Lake

There are three important pioneers of Saranac Lake Village. Jacob Smith Moody was the first settler of Saranac Lake. He was born in Keene, New Hampshire in the year 1787. Moody settled in Saranac Lake in 1819. He had seven children: six boys and one girl. He died in Saranac Lake Village in 1863. Another pioneer was Pliny Miller and many believed the village grew around him. He was a close friend of Jacob Moody and settled in the village in 1822. Miller was born in 1775 in Sand Lake, located in Rensselaer County. He had eight children: five girls and three boys. He died in Saranac Lake Village in 1859. And the third pioneer was Milote Baker. He came from Keeseville in 1852. Baker was born in New Bedford, Massachusetts in 1806. He died in 1875. Baker was the Head of the Commissary Department at the Sing Sing Prison; he became the first postmaster of Saranac Lake.

Saranac Lake has the unique feature of having dry air. The land itself consists of extreme sandiness and porousness of soil. There is a lack of humidity. Remarkably papers and books can be left in a summer camp all winter without showing a trace of dampness in the spring. The lack of humidity robs the cold of the winter of its sting and the heat of the summer of its sappiness (History of the Adirondacks by Alfred L. Donaldson). It is intensely cold in the winter; temperatures could be forty degrees to fifty degrees below zero.

During the time span of 1855-1890 everything depended on the stagecoach. This was the era just prior to the "opening" of the frontier. The stagecoach carried people, parcels, mail and news. The main stagecoach routes were from Elizabethtown to Keeseville to Ausable Forks. A famous visitor to Saranac Lake was Robert Louis Stevenson. He visited during the winter of 1887-1888. He mainly came since he was suffering from pulmonary tuberculosis. But he became worsened and caught cold. During his stay he wrote a series of twelve papers; eleven of the twelve writings he completed while in Saranac Lake for the periodical "Scribner's Magazine."

SKETCH #3:

Adirondack Lore

The word Adirondacks means "tree eaters." This was a word commonly used by the Iroquois. The Adirondacks is a group of mountains in northeastern New York State. Samuel de Champlain may be the one credited with discovering the Adirondacks in 1608. The Indians never made any part of the Adirondack Park their permanent home. Though North Elba may have been a possible settlement of Indians. The burial place of John Brown may be possible Indian settlements.

The Adirondack Park is prime muskrat habitat. There are over four thousand lakes, ponds, swamps and bogs. There are 30,000 miles of rivers, streams and brooks. The Adirondack wilderness is one of trees: sugar maples, black maples, striped maples, red maples, silver maples, mountain maples, swamp maples, black oaks, northern red oaks, chestnut oaks, bur oaks, swamp white oaks, white oaks, American beeches, willows of all species, deciduous trees along with eastern hemlocks, Scotch pines, white pines, pitch pines, red pines, and jack pines.

There are red, black, white and Norway spruces too.

The Adirondacks is approximately six million acres. 2.6 million acres are the Adirondack Forest Preserve. The other 3.4 million acres is private property of one sort or another. It is about the size of the state of New Hampshire. There are roughly two thousand peaks that qualify as mountains. More than forty are higher than four thousand feet; these are known as the High Peaks. Two of the mountains, Marcy and Algonquin, have summits greater than five thousand feet.

Algonquin is a mountain in Essex County. It bears the name of one of the most widely known hotels in the Adirondacks. The hotel was converted to a sanatorium for tuberculosis treatment. It closed in 1924. A horrific wildfire took place on Noonmark Mountain in September 1999.

Marcy is the highest mountain in the state of New York. Mount Marcy was made known by a historical event in 1901. President McKinley was shot by an anarchist in Buffalo on September 6. 1901. Theodore Roosevelt, the vice president, made his way to Buffalo and remained there until he was assured that President McKinley was not in danger. Roosevelt then went to the Adirondacks to join his family. On September 13th, Roosevelt and some friends made an ascent of Mount Marcy. They reached the summit, stayed for about fifteen minutes and then began their descent. As they stopped along the trail for lunch, a guide came up the path to deliver a telegram to Mr. Roosevelt which told him that President McKinley's condition had worsened. But Roosevelt was unable to arrive back before McKinley died.

SKETCH #4:

Crown Point

The British constructed the Fort of Crown Point. It was an ambitious project. Long before the Revolutionary War, the British and the French claimed Crown Point in the struggle for a North American Empire. There were four failed campaigns to oust the French between 1755 and 1758. It was not until 1759 that the abandoned French Fort St. Frederic was taken over by the British.

In 1775, at the outbreak of the revolutionary war, the rebellious colonists captured the fort and secured sorely needed cannons. Crown Point was occupied by British General John Burgoyne's army in 1777. Despite loss of territory elsewhere, Burgoyne's troops continued to hold Crown Point until 1781. It was not until the end of the war that the Americans reoccupied the area and regained control of navigation of Lake Champlain.

Today the ruins at Crown Point have been preserved, substantially unchanged. The landmark exhibits the superior architectural and archeological example of 18th century military engineering. The Crown Point fortress had an elaborate wooden bridge and gate, an officers' barracks, a village consisting of a few dozen buildings including homes, a tavern, an apothecary, a store and a blacksmith shop, along with well-constructed walls and bombproofs. The land approaches to the fort were protected by smaller fortifications called redoubts. Some of the architectural design still provides protection from the elements today.

SKETCH #5:

Keene

Keene is contained within a hundred and sixty five square mile area. Keene is approximately fifteen miles outside of Lake Placid, the home of the 1932 and 1980 Olympics. It is a rural community where families worked at the saw mills and grist mills during the nineteenth century and early twentieth century. Keene is abundant with hiking trails, including Mount Marcy, the highest peak at 5,344 feet, in New York State. Keene was formed in 1808.

Keene has often been referred to as the Home of the High Peaks. People throughout the region are quite familiar with the 46ers; these are the mountains of at least four thousand feet in ascent. Each mountain has its own unique background. Keene is located along Route 73 and is a main thoroughfare to Lake Placid, Saranac Lake and other destinations.

Over the years the economy of Keene has adapted to the changing times. A major addition was the Stewart's Convenience Shop. There also have been changes due to the aftermath of Hurricane Sandy in 2012. There are also various quaint shops, a renovated fire house, a public library and post office along with the town hall and art studio.

RESOURCES

Koehler, Steven A. (Dr.) and Wecht, Cyril (Dr.) <u>Postmortem: Establishing the Cause of Death</u>, Firefly Books, 2006.

Farnsworth, Cheri L., <u>Adirondack Enigma: The Depraved Intellect and Mysterious Life of North Country Wife Killer Henry DeBosnys</u>, The History Press, 2010.

www.dec.ny.gov

<u>Town of Jay: Planning Report</u>, Essex County Planning Office for Town of Jay, NY, August 1980.

"Fred A. Torrance: His Life, Times and Philosophy," published by Isabelle Torrance.

Bernstein, Burton, <u>The Sticks: A Profile of Essex County, New York</u>, Vail-Ballou Press, Inc., 1971 (1972).

Schneider, Paul, <u>The Adirondacks: A History of America's First Wilderness</u>, Henry Holt and Company, Inc., 1997 (1st edition).

Donaldson, Alfred L., <u>A History of the Adirondacks</u>, Purple Mountain Press, Ltd., 1996 (Second Printing: 2002).

Adirondack History Center Museum (Essex County Historical Society), Elizabethtown, N.Y.

<u>www.nysparks.com/historic-sites</u> (Crown Point Historic Site).